"I've been hire

"Then you're going to have to make it, and you better do it good. Because I'm not leaving without her."

Bridge lunged. Wendy ducked, dropping to the ground on her knees, then somersaulted backward, landing on her feet and slicing him again in the arm as he charged forward. Another superficial wound, but it would burn like fresh pale skin under the July sun.

That put some growl into his bear.

She went for him again. But he saw it coming and sidestepped her. Lightning fast but still restraining all his power; that punch of Bridge's full force would have knocked her smooth out. Before she could shake off the mountain spinning before her, he lunged for the gun.

Gunfire erupted.

She fell backward, stunned. He would. He would put a bullet right through her. She never thought it'd come to this. Then he tackled her. "Stay down."

"What?" She was loopy from the sucker punch.

"I didn't fire that shot. *You think I'd shoot you?*"

Jessica R. Patch lives in the Mid-South, where she pens inspirational contemporary romance and romantic suspense novels. When she's not hunched over her laptop or going on adventurous trips with willing friends in the name of research, you can find her watching way too much Netflix with her family and collecting recipes for amazing dishes she'll probably never cook. To learn more about Jessica, please visit her at jessicarpatch.com.

Visit the Author Profile page at LoveInspired.com for more titles.

ATTEMPTED MOUNTAIN ABDUCTION

JESSICA R. PATCH

LOVE INSPIRED SUSPENSE
INSPIRATIONAL ROMANCE

 **LOVE INSPIRED® SUSPENSE**
INSPIRATIONAL ROMANCE

Recycling programs for this product may not exist in your area.

ISBN-13: 978-1-335-63876-2

Attempted Mountain Abduction

Copyright © 2025 by Jessica R. Patch

Love Inspired
22 Adelaide St. West, 41st Floor
Toronto, Ontario M5H 4E3, Canada
www.LoveInspired.com

Printed in Lithuania

MIX
Paper | Supporting responsible forestry
FSC® C021394

For if they fall, the one will lift up his fellow:
but woe to him that is alone when he falleth;
for he hath not another to help him up.
—*Ecclesiastes* 4:10

To my son-in-love, Nathan, who is a brilliant fisherman. I threw in fishing just for you. We love having you in our family and are always thankful for you. Just know, I write suspense, so I'm well adept in hiding bodies. Keep making our baby happy. ;)

Special thanks to my agent, Rachel Kent; my editor, Shana Asaro; and my craft partner, Susan L. Tuttle. My books would not be what they are without you wonderful women!

ONE

Bridge Spencer stepped onto his cabin's porch, shivering at the biting cold, but something icier hovered in the January wind and scraped his nerves like jagged icicles. The sun had dipped below the mountains a half an hour ago. He shouldn't be drinking coffee this late, but he needed the jolt of caffeine. He frowned, unable to place the sensation of danger lurking in the thick forest that surrounded him here at The Great Smoky Mountains Riders Camp—a kids' camp that lasted two weeks during winter break and taught children how to ride horses.

Maybe it was the case he was working, now that he was employed by Spears & Bow Bodyguards International. Axel Spears had been on him for over a year to take a job with his company, and finally, this past Christmas, he'd done it. He was now officially part of a bodyguard agency made up of former law enforcement agents. He and Axel had been friends since their time at the FBI Academy in Quantico, even though their work in the Bureau had led them in different directions.

When things had gone sideways for Bridge three years ago—when he'd lost a boy only eight years old and one of his best agents to an undercover op that imploded—he'd never forgiven himself. Resigned the following day and went home to his family in Texas. Home to his family ranch and to work for his eldest brother, Stone, who ran Spencer Aftermath Recovery and Grief Counseling Services, which cleaned up scenes after crimes and accidents and provided counseling services for loved ones.

Never once had he discussed what transpired that sent him running with this tail tucked between his legs. And he never spoke of the devastation that happened two weeks later at Christmas when Wendy, his fiancée, mailed him a Dear John letter and disappeared. He would be a liar if he didn't wonder if this was punishment by God for losing a child and a friend. He had been responsible for them. For the entire operation.

His anxiety might be heightened because he was now on a new undercover mission, his first assignment with Spears & Bow, tasked with protecting a ten-year-old girl. Molly Wingbender was only two years older than Levi James, the boy he'd lost. The boy he'd vowed to protect and return from his kidnappers. The boy and family he'd failed.

Axel may have deliberately thrown Bridge into the deep end to help him face his fear, but Bridge suspected his expertise with horses, thanks to being raised on a ranch, and his undercover experience simply made him the best choice.

Dread had pooled in his gut. Men were after Molly. Her father, Charlie Wingbender, had been a mogul in Silicon Valley and died three years ago. His older brother David had taken guardianship of Molly and put her in a private boarding school in New Hampshire. But then an attempt to kidnap her was made, and David believed it had to do with the top-secret project Charlie had been working on before he died. The Mask program, which had something to do with deepfakes, but that's about all Bridge and the team knew. He hired Spears & Bow to accompany her to the horse farm, hoping no one would find her in the hills of Tennessee. After her two weeks here, Bridge would accompany her back to school while they hoped the threats were neutralized.

The problem was, they didn't know where the threat originated, and if they wanted to kidnap Molly to force David into finishing his brother's work, they were in trouble. David lacked his brother's tech skills and had no clue where Charlie stored the coding for his project on deepfakes.

Presently, deepfakes were glorified photoshopping and used a form of artificial intelligence called deep learning to make images of fake events, hence the name deepfake. If someone wanted to put new words in a politician's mouth, star in their favorite movie, or dance like a pro, it would be easy to do in a deepfake. But Charlie Wingbender's project would allow someone to hack into live events and create a real-time deepfake. Any corrupt person, government or entity could turn the world upside down with this kind of technology. Bridge could scarcely imagine what would happen if the wrong people got their hands on this. They could hack the president's live speech and make changes with no one being the wiser. Videos could be made of people committing crimes they didn't, but it would be near impossible to prove otherwise. It could be dangerous, and deadly criminals wanted it—enough that they probably killed Charlie for it, only to realize the project was missing pieces of code.

Bridge's coffee was now cold. He checked his watch. He had fifteen minutes until he had to be down at the mess hall for dinner, and then he was giving an expert lesson on mounting a horse and horse safety. The camp directors had been informed who Bridge was, and they had assigned Molly to all his groups and one-on-one sessions with Bridge. The only downside was he couldn't be with her 24/7, so he watched from a distance when he couldn't be near.

He leaned on the wooden post of his cabin's porch railing. Snow was coming soon. Living in Texas hadn't given him much opportunity for snow, but he'd lived in Colorado for a few years, working out of the FBI field office in Denver. He was no stranger to it and loved it. Fresh and pure. He even loved the powdery crunch under his feet, stomping around in it. Didn't much like the ice though.

"Hey," a deep voice broke him from his thoughts. Matthew LaSalle, another camp horse guide, approached from two cabins down. Bridge's soft porch light surrounded Matt in an eerie glow. "Heading to the mess hall for dinner. You coming?" Matt was pretty cool. A few years younger than Bridge's thirty-seven years. He carried a southern accent, but Bridge wasn't sure where he hailed from. Never asked. He was here to do a job. Safeguarding Molly Wingbender, who—

He glanced at his watch again. Archer had provided it for him. It linked to Molly's secret GPS tracker. She was still in her cabin she shared with seven other girls. Their cabin mom was Sandra Bachman. She was someone Bridge had done thorough recon on since she was with Molly most, second to Bridge.

"Yeah. Moving slow today. The cold's in my bones."

Matt chuckled. "I hear that. Blizzard's coming tomorrow morning. Temperatures are going to plummet over the next twelve hours. You see that on the news?"

"No."

"Could be the worst we've seen at this lower elevation since '93. Or it could be nothing. They don't really know." He waved off the idea with an attitude of a man who'd spent a lot of time outside.

"What happens if we're snowed in?"

"Nothing." He laughed. "That's the point. Some parents are flying in helicopters to chopper the kids out just in case. Rich kids. Must be nice, right?"

"Must be," Bridge muttered. He hadn't grown up with a silver spoon in his mouth. But he had nothing against folks who had more. And he certainly didn't hold it against the children. "Will we shut down?"

"We'll be snowed in with the kids. That'll be great." Sarcasm dripped from his lips. "We have generators but kids become bored easy. They're paying me to teach them how to ride horses, not entertain them any other way, so I'm crossing my fingers that the blizzard stays at Dairy Queen. Am I right?"

Bridge grinned. "Right."

Matt saluted and hunched against the bitter wind as he made his way to the mess hall.

After grabbing his gloves, Carhartt jacket, backpack and knit cap, he jogged toward the smell of savory garlic and onion. Roast was on the menu tonight. Inside the cafeteria, kids sat at long tables eating family style. The chatter was deafening as they had over one hundred and fifty campers from ages ten to seventeen. Cabin moms and dads sat at the tables, keeping kids semi-under control while the directors of the camp sat at the table closest to the kitchen.

Bridge scanned the tables. Molly was particular about the seating arrangement. She liked the same table and space on the bench each day. She was quite vocal if another camper beat her to the seat. In fact, Molly liked everything just so, from her schedule to wearing the same colors. She loved yellow, and she wore a different variation of it each day. But tonight she wasn't at her table and her space on the bench. He found her cabin mom.

"Hey, Sandra," Bridge said.

With bright blue eyes, Sandra looked up at

him, her long blond hair neatly tied in a pony-tail. Her toothy smile met his. "Hi, Bridge. What can I do for you?"

"I'm wondering where Molly is." He checked his tracker app. Archer Crow, his other boss at Spears & Bow, had sent a GPS locator, which Bridge had placed inside Molly's camp bracelet she had to wear 24/7. Archer was the co-founder of the agency, but he was never around in person. Only on Zoom calls, and his background was hidden using green screen technology. Bridge's other two team members—Libby Winters and Amber Rathbone—knew as little about him as Bridge. But Axel would be aware of Archer's bizarre behavior and Bridge trusted Axel.

"She wasn't feeling well. Nurse Angie is seeing to her."

"Not feeling well how?" Was she just under the weather? Or had someone poisoned her? Every dangerous scenario played in his head.

"Headache I think. Nothing to worry about. It's been a long day." She touched his hand and then he noticed the flicker in her eye. Oh, that was the last thing he needed. A cabin mom with a crush.

He looked down at his phone. The tracker showed she was no longer in the cabin. She was moving. No doubt toward the nurses' cabin, which was on the north end of the campground next to the administrative building.

"Right. Thanks," he muttered and blew out of the cafeteria. He'd feel better once he checked on Molly. Checking the tracker again, he frowned. Her movement wasn't going toward the nurses' cabin. It was moving west.

West was toward the woods.

This must be why he'd been filled with foreboding since he'd woken before dawn. His first case on the new job and his client was on the move away from the camp. No way she'd taken a wrong turn. Molly had the entire campground memorized from studying the map so she wouldn't end up lost. She liked knowing where everything was. She knew the place almost as well as Bridge.

So why would she and the nurse be going in the opposite direction?

Maybe the nurse wasn't truly a nurse, like Bridge wasn't a genuine horse guide.

He followed their movement, relieved by its lack of speed. They were on foot. Using the sliver of moonlight as a guide, he rushed past the cabin and beyond a thicket of trees that expanded into the mountains. He wasn't sure where they were headed. The unfamiliar terrain might lead to a road where a vehicle waited to whisk Molly away. A million deadly possibilities echoed out in his head, but he forced himself to remain cool, calm and collected.

This was not Levi James.

He pushed into the tightly woven trees, brush, pine needles and gnarly roots jutting from the ground, slowing him. The brittle branches scraped against one another as the wind picked up. Molly was about fifty yards ahead. He darted forward, his heart rate spiking. She wasn't as fast, and he quickly gained ground.

A dark-clad figure rounded a tree. Tall. Slender. Holding Molly's hand and a flashlight. Leading her away from camp. Bridge's lungs constricted. He couldn't fire a shot. If he missed and it ricocheted off a tree, he risked Molly being hit. Plus, whoever had her was smart, keeping to the trees as shields.

"I need to go to the bathroom," Molly boomed. The child had one decibel by which she operated. Loud. He heard no fear in her voice but irritation rang through. This person had interrupted her routine, and she was not a happy camper. Quite literally.

The figure paused and pointed to the bushes about five feet away in a dense patch of brush. Now was his chance as Molly distanced herself and disappeared into the shrubs and fallen trunks.

Bridge silently maneuvered behind the trees

until he was right behind the figure. A runner's build. Well, he would not run from Bridge. Springing from the trees, Bridge launched himself at the kidnapper, wrapping his hands around the man's throat.

But the dude was fast. And strong. He bent forward and dropped to his knees, throwing Bridge off balance.

"What's going on over there?" Molly shouted from the bushes. "I'm trying to do my business in privacy. You do know that word, don't you? It means the state or condition of being free from being observed or disturbed by other people. Verbatim the Oxford Languages dictionary. You can Google it."

Oh yeah, the kid was a literal know-it-all, even in a crisis.

The figure in the ski mask swept Bridge's leg out from under him and he hit the hard packed, cold ground with a thud. Then the attacker was on him with a knife at his throat. Darkness hovered and Bridge couldn't make out the eyes, but he knew that move. Bend. Drop. *The Karate Kid*—a reference to the "sweep the leg" maneuver from the movie. It gave time to incapacitate the attacker. It was a move he himself had taught federal agents.

Whoever was kidnapping Molly had received training from Bridge.

He brought up his hand and wrapped it around the assailant's wrist. Slender. Small. Delicate. Not a man.

A woman.

That's when he caught the handle of the knife blade, made from mother-of-pearl.

Only one person he knew had that kind of blade.

His heart stuttered and stumbled, and his throat squeezed tight.

"Wendy?"

Wendy Dawson froze as she hovered over the man trying to steal Molly Wingbender from her. That voice was familiar, lapping like warm waters around her heart. A voice unheard in three years. Three years in isolation, investigating the murder of Charlie Wingbender, hunting down the missing pieces of code left on flash drives and trying to take down the monster who had forced her to abandon everything and everyone she cared about.

Including Bridge Spencer. The only man she'd ever loved.

"Bridge?" She lowered the weapon about to slice through his carotid and grabbed the flashlight, shining it in his face. His rugged beautiful face registered confusion and shock. This *would* be a serious shock to the system. What was he doing here? "Why are you after me?" Every other agency seemed to be. FBI might as well be too.

"Because you're kidnapping a child." He gripped her shoulders and forced her body off of his. She landed on the cold ground with a thud.

Crunching and cracking echoed as Molly emerged from the brush, a scowl on her otherwise sweet cherub face. Her dark long hair surrounded her shoulders, framing her heart-shaped face, and her equally dark eyes met Wendy's. "Why are you wrestling Mr. Bridge?"

"You know him?" Confusion overwhelmed her. If Bridge was on a covert mission following Wendy, why did Molly know him? Wendy had only arrived tonight after discovering intel that Molly was in danger. She had incapacitated the nurse back at Molly's cabin, but the woman was surely awake by now and in no serious pain.

"He's my horse guide," Molly replied. "Did you know surveys suggest that roughly one in every hundred children experience a stranger trying to lure them away in order to do them harm? I read that on an abduction website after they killed my dad."

Of course she did. The child's mind was a holding cell for knowledge. "Horse guide?" Wendy asked.

Bridge sprang to his feet and raked a hand

through his thick brown hair. He'd normally kept it short, but he'd grown it out some since last she saw him. Not long like his brother Rhode. Just enough to show the natural wave. And he'd grown a beard. His amber eyes met Wendy's. A million questions whirled in her mind like a tornado. "I'm Molly's horse guide and instructor for the winter break. And who are you to her?"

He was no horse guide in Tennessee. Which meant...he was undercover. Made sense. Bridge recruited and trained FBI agents for undercover work in the Critical Incidence Response Group (CIRG). He ran missions all the time. They must know Molly had been compromised. Was that all they knew?

"I'm a friend taking her somewhere safe." That's all he needed to know about her relationship with the Wingbender family at this point. The less he knew the safer he would be. But he was here so he might know much more.

"Sure you are." He turned to Molly. "I want you to walk toward me." Bridge positioned himself between her and Wendy.

"Bridge, I'm friend, not foe."

His eyes narrowed. "You are far from a friend."

Molly moved behind Bridge and he pulled a gun, aiming it right between Wendy's eyes. Did he have the moxie to shoot her? The woman he'd dipped a knee to when he'd pledged his undying love for her and slipped a pear-shaped carat diamond on her left ring finger? Could these past three years have callused his heart enough to run a bullet through her brain? Because she was sure she couldn't do it to him. But if he fought her, she'd have no choice but to engage. She gripped her knife.

"You should know never to bring a knife to a gunfight, Wendy." His eyes radiated a challenge.

"I'm taking the child," she said, her tone resolute. "And you'll have to kill me to stop me. Can you do that, Bridge? Can you pull that trigger in cold blood?"

"That's all I have left, Wendy. Cold blood. Cold heart. I have you to thank for that." His tone was icy and bitter, like the wind whistling like a train through the barren trees. At the moment, she didn't have time to feel guilty. She'd nurse those wounds later when she was alone with nothing but her burning thoughts that plagued her like gnats on a summer day.

She gripped her knife, and his eyes followed her movement. "You won't win. Don't do it, Wendy," he warned, his voice low and menacing.

"Am I about to be a hostage?" Molly asked. "Hostages are sometimes the only way to enact a plan. What is the plan, Mr. Bridge?"

"No one is a hostage and this—" he pointed from himself to Wendy repeatedly "—isn't going to go any further." He held Wendy's gaze. "Do not make me hurt you."

"Keep talking big, Bridge. I'll be the one doing the hurting if you don't hand over that child." She returned his warning with a stronger one. She wasn't afraid of Bridge Spencer. But that was only because at one time he'd loved her. He never would have hurt her. Now, she was no longer the object of his affection. She was the aftermath of destruction and brokenness. And she wasn't stupid enough not to know Bridge was dangerous. Lethal. He moved like lightning and he never struck twice. No need. That had been his nickname in the Bureau. Agent Lightning.

But the CIA's best had trained Wendy. She wasn't a waif. She wasn't the weaker sex. And he should be wary of her too. By the calculation in his eyes, he wasn't underestimating her. She wasn't sure if she should be proud or terrified. If he was calculating her moves, then he was also counter-calculating. They were like living chess pieces and one of them was going to have to call a checkmate.

The question was which one of them would make the first move? She'd technically already struck blood when she'd left him three years ago right before Christmas with nothing but a cowardly letter. But it had been for his own protection. If he came at her with fangs bared now, it would only be in retaliation for what she'd already done.

"Is this a standoff?" Molly asked. "According to the Oxford Languages, a standoff is a stalemate or deadlock between two equally matched opponents in a dispute or conflict."

Spot on, kiddo.

Wendy was taking this child. Now. Molly was in grave danger and not from her. She had to move her somewhere safe, and now that Bridge was somehow involved, he was in potential danger too, which meant he needed to be as far away from Wendy as possible for his own safety, and if hurting him was the only way, she'd have to do so. It was time to take the chance that their past would keep him from shooting her dead.

Suddenly, she dropped to her knees and thrust forward, swiping the knife upward, hitting Bridge in the side. A strategic flesh wound. Quickly, she rolled to the side as he winced, shock registering on his face. *Strike two, Bridge. I'm sorry.*

She sprang to her feet and round kicked him, knocking him into the tree and the gun from his hand. Rookie move losing the gun. He was rusty and that also confused her. But Bridge had to go down and out. At least long enough to give her and the kid a head start out of the mountains.

"Molly, start running that way. Now." But before she could point the direction, Bridge tackled Wendy with a force that a defensive lineman would be proud of. The impact on the ground rattled her bones. He wasn't holding back now. He was in this for all it was worth.

Not waiting for direction, Molly shot into the woods.

Bridge hollered for her to stop, but she didn't. The girl kept running.

Okay, time to bloody up my former fiancé. Not a thought she ever expected to think. But she had to incapacitate him and catch up to Molly before the bad guys intercepted her. She didn't know who they were. No names. No faces. Ghosts. She was fighting the wind.

And Bridge.

"Do you think I'd kill that girl?" She raised a knee to nail him in the groin, but he blocked her. Guess he was finally remembering how to fight. Too bad. He held her down, using both arms to pin her to the cold earth.

She spit in his face, shocking him, then raised up and head butted him. His arms released her and Wendy jabbed his left jaw. Once. Twice. Quick succession. She got to her feet.

He *was* holding back. Because she was a woman or because she was Wendy—who he once loved? Maybe both. "Don't make me hurt you, Wendy."

His side bled, and sweat ran down his scruffy face, despite the cold.

"Let me take her and go then."

"I can't do that. I've been hired to protect her," Bridge said.

"Then you're going to have to hurt me, Bridge, and you better do it good. Because I'm not leaving without her."

He lunged. She ducked, dropping to the ground on her knees, then somersaulted backward, landing on her feet and slicing him again in the arm as he charged forward. Another superficial wound, but it would burn like fresh pale skin under the July sun.

That put some growl into his bear.

She came for him again to punch the spot near his carotid. One chop and he would go down and out for at least five minutes. That's all she needed. But he saw it coming and sidestepped her, then clipped her jaw with his fist, rattling her brain and sending spots in front of her eyes. He was lightning fast but still restraining all his power; that punch at Bridge's full force would have knocked her smooth out. Before she could shake off the mountain spinning before her, he lunged for the gun.

Gunfire erupted.

She fell backward, stunned. He would do it. He would put a bullet right through her. She never thought it'd come to this. Then he tackled her. "Stay down."

"What?" She was loopy from the sucker punch.

"I didn't fire that shot. You think I'd shoot you?"

He'd just knocked the ever lovin' stuffin' from her brain. Yeah. She expected the brass next. Actually, she'd expected a harder hit.

"Who's with you?"

Wendy shoved him off her. "I've been trying to tell you. I'm here to save the child. Not kidnap her or kill her. Now let's go find her or she's in real trouble." No way to keep him out of this mess now. She'd simply have to protect them both.

Another shot fired, spraying bark from the pine tree above them. They rolled together toward the brush where Molly had been earlier.

Cold ground at her back, Bridge's granite chest tight against her, they landed in the thicket. "Who is after her? After you?" he asked.

"I'm not sure. Now's not the time. We have to call a truce. Let me run with Molly and you head them off."

"Not a chance."

"Fine. Then it's your funeral."

They rolled to a stop, her back on the ground, his weight heavy on top of her. Protecting her. Shielding her. After she'd sliced his flesh. He might need a stitch or two. Having been trained since she was twenty-one years old, she knew how to make someone feel pain and how to end them. Bridge would survive.

His Adam's apple bobbed as he swallowed hard. "Okay," he murmured. "Truce, but I don't trust you and if for one second I think you're turning on me… Wendy, so help me I won't hold back. I won't stop. You understand?"

Bridge was forewarning her that a jab to her jaw would be nothing. "Fair enough."

He rose from her and helped her up. Then they rushed through the thicket, keeping to the trees. Wendy hoped Molly hadn't gotten too far away. Or worse—into the hands of merciless killers.

TWO

Bridge raced through the woods, Wendy at his side and his mind reeling. He hadn't had time to process that the woman he'd loved was here in front of his very eyes. And knocking the junk right out of him. It had pained him to inflict any kind of pain on her, but she'd given him no choice. Bridge had never met a more headstrong woman and fierce fighter. Wendy was a force to be reckoned with and to be feared. Even by men who outweighed her by a hundred pounds, which he absolutely did.

If she'd wanted to kill him, he'd be dead. She'd gone easy with the knife, purposefully striking areas that wouldn't damage organs or hit arteries. But she'd only play nice for so long. And it appeared she was telling the truth about helping not hurting Molly. Not that Wendy would ever harm a child, but he wasn't sure what her plan for Molly was. She said she was there to protect her, but how?

All Bridge cared about was the kid. Spears & Bow had given him an order. The first one since he'd lost little Levi, and he would not fail. If that meant popping Wendy's chin with his fist, then he'd do it. And if it meant they'd come to blows later… Well…he didn't want to think about what it might come to. Now he just wanted to find Molly, escape the sniper and find a safe place to figure all this out. He had so many questions.

"She's up ahead," Wendy said, not winded by their trek or the earlier scuffle.

Shots sounded again.

"We're leading them to her!" Bridge couldn't let them hurt the child.

"Well, we can't leave her. It's me they know they have to kill to catch her. Split up. You go for Molly and I'll lead them away. You have a phone on you?"

"Yeah, but the service is shoddy out here. We *are* in the mountains."

"Don't take that mocking tone with me, Bridge. I'll lay you out right here and now. I can track your phone if it's the same number."

"You'll be putting yourself directly in the line of fire."

"But Molly would be safe." She paused. "You'd be safe." Her voice softened at the last statement and his heart stuttered. "It's our only shot, and you know it."

Another bullet fired and missed Wendy's head by a hair's breadth. She ducked and rolled behind a tree. "Go. Now. I'll find you. I promise."

"You've made promises before. Ones like *I'll love you all my life.* And *we're in it together forever.*"

Her blue eyes met his. "I will find you."

The words struck a chord in his chest. Bridge believed this promise, but only because she wanted Molly, and he had no clue why. "Okay. Be safe." But he already knew she would be. He trusted no one more to take care of herself than Wendy Dawson. He bolted out of the trees, a shot firing in his direction. Dirt sprayed next to his feet, but he didn't return fire. He had one gun. One cartridge. No backups. Using trees for shields, he kept running.

Someone fired another shot, but they didn't aim it at him. Had they followed Wendy, intent on killing her? Bridge still wasn't sure what Wendy was doing here, but he was sure of one thing: she was a liar and he didn't trust her. His mistrust had nothing to do with her job description, which required deception. His own past job with the FBI had required him to go under cover with fake identities in order to infiltrate evil. To stop it. Capture it.

Who knows? Maybe Wendy had become so adept at lying that when she'd told him she wanted to leave the field in order to move to Texas with him and make a home and a family—something she knew couldn't be done as a field operator—she'd actually believed her own lie.

But then to deliver a letter that she was leaving and couldn't be a wife and mom… That had been the real Wendy. The woman who wanted to be in fieldwork and brave villains and death. But not to face Bridge to tell him she didn't love him and wanted her career instead was the coward's way out.

His grief had morphed into hurt, then anger and now just the sour taste of bitterness, knowing he had no say in her choice. They could have made it work. They'd been together two years, both of them working full-time in consuming careers but finding patches of time for themselves. She was going to finish one last classified assignment that would take maybe two weeks, three tops, and then it would be just them.

That never happened.

No matter now. What mattered was keeping Molly safe and he couldn't be certain Wendy had the child's best interest at heart. She definitely hadn't had his.

Molly hunkered in a bramble bush, a frown puckering her face. "I never received my ibuprofen and I still have a headache."

Bridge sighed. Molly didn't have the sense to

be afraid, and that benefited them. Molly was neurodivergent. That was clear from the moment he met her. She was brutally honest, rigid but kind and funny, though he was certain she never intended to be. And she was off-the-charts intelligent. She might be a fabulous analyst for the government one day.

"I have some in my backpack. Let's reach a safer location. Can you make it?"

"Do I have a choice?"

"Not really." Bridge had learned to be brutally honest in return. Molly appreciated straightforwardness.

"Are we going to die like my dad?" she asked and pulled her knit cap farther down on her brow.

"No. The woman who took you is a powerful lady. And I'm no joke either."

"I agree. You're not funny."

Not what he meant but… "Sorry to hear that, Moll."

"Molly. My name is Molly, not Moll. And your name isn't a name. It's a noun. A bridge is a structure carrying a road, path, railroad or canal across a river, ravine, road, railroad or other obstacle. That's from the Oxford Languages."

Bridge smirked and then put his finger to his mouth for her to be quiet. She silenced immediately and put her finger on her mouth. He focused on listening. Birds rattling brittle branches. Wind whistling in the trees. No gunfire. No sound of running or disturbances on the forest floor.

Going back toward the camp would intersect them with the people after them, and Bridge didn't know who they were. For all he knew, it was someone who had also infiltrated the camp. The weather forecast predicted an approaching blizzard. He had no camping supplies and spending the night in the open with the elements was a death trap. No good options here.

"Come on. We're going to move down the mountain. We might find a town." He checked his cell phone. No bars. As he figured.

"What town?" she asked and clambered to her feet. Her nose and cheeks were bright pink. Wendy had made sure Molly wore her parka, gloves and warm clothes. She also carried a yellow backpack, he noticed now that he was paying more attention. Guess Wendy had intended to trek out of the mountain, which meant she'd studied the rugged terrain, likely had a map and a plan.

"I don't know."

"Then how do you know there is a town?"

"I'm guessing."

"Hypothermia is most likely at very cold temperatures, but it can occur even at cool temperatures above forty degrees Fahrenheit if a person becomes chilled from rain, sweat or submersion in cold water. That's from the USDA Forest Service. It's forty-two degrees." Molly eyed him, waiting on his honesty. "Guessing isn't accuracy. Guessing means estimate or suppose, something without sufficient information to be sure of being correct. That's from the Oxford Languages. The temperature is fact."

Well, what did he say to that? Nothing like having a doomsdayer with him. "We'll head down the mountain until she catches up to us and she'll have a foolproof plan. I hope." Not that he and Molly would follow it. Not until he could be sure Wendy was trustworthy.

"Hope isn't accurate either."

Bridge rubbed his brow bone and waited for the definition, which quickly came.

"Hope in Jesus is foolproof, Molly. So I'm going to put my hope to keep us safe in Him."

"How is hope in Jesus foolproof, Mr. Bridge?" Molly asked, innocent eyes full of expectancy.

"Because the Bible says hope in Him never disappoints." He held up his finger. "We'll talk more about it later. Right now, we need to find a new safe place."

"Okay. But I won't forget you said we could talk about it later, and if you don't, I'll remind you." She shoved a tuff of long hair up under her knit cap.

"I know you will." Bridge chuckled under his breath. This little girl was awesome and frustrating at the same time. A lot like Wendy. He silently prayed she was safe and would indeed find them. "You cold?"

"That's not a smart question. I told you. It's forty-two degrees." She cocked her head, and he nodded.

"Let's keep moving." He went to pat her shoulder, but she didn't care to be touched and if one did, they needed permission. He'd learned that the first day of camp, which had been one week ago tomorrow. Saturday. Instead, he pointed in the direction he wanted her to go. "Stay near me. Bad guys are looking for you, but me and Miss Wendy—the woman helping us—" he hoped "—are going to keep you safe."

"I'm not afraid."

"I know. Just informing you. I know you like to be informed of things."

She nodded once. "My dad liked that too. He always had a big whiteboard with our schedules. I liked that."

From the background information he'd read through, Molly's mom had passed away from a car accident when she was only two. Charlie had raised her, but she'd had a nanny who watched her most days because of his long hours on his research projects. Charlie's brother, David, was the only next of kin and had two grown children. Becoming guardian of Molly had been a big disruption, and he'd sent her to boarding school. He said to keep her off-the-grid, but Bridge had his doubts. David didn't seem like a man who wanted to be bothered with a child and Bridge believed that was part of his motive in sending her away.

They pushed through the woods, and surprisingly his stomach growled. Guess the body wanted what the body wanted. "Are you hungry?"

Molly shook her head. "No. I was given a granola bar after we left the cabin. You know by the lady who beat you up."

"I wouldn't say she beat me up."

"She cut you up then. You're still bleeding. An adult will have approximately 1.2 to 1.5 gallons, or ten units, of blood in their body. Blood is approximately ten percent of an adult's weight. I read that from the Red Cross's website once. After my dad died. I found him and he'd lost a lot of blood. I wondered how much. Now I know."

She said it so matter-of-fact. At seven she'd wondered how much blood he'd lost? "I'm sorry about your dad."

"Why? Did you kill him?" she asked and kept moving ahead.

"No. No, I didn't. I just feel bad that you lost your dad."

She paused and looked at him. Her brow knit. "I didn't lose him. He died."

"Right. That's true. But I feel bad he died. I know you loved him."

She smiled just a little. "I still love him. He said I had an enormous beautiful brain, but he never saw my brain, so he couldn't know if it was beautiful or not."

Bridge chuckled. "Good point. My dad died. He had a heart attack. One of my sisters died too. Paisley. Someone killed her, like someone killed your father. I love them still too. It makes me sad that they're dead." He was going to say gone, but she'd argue they weren't gone, but buried.

"I'm not sure what sorrow is. I know it's sadness, and sadness is sorrow, but I don't know the word to explain the emotion."

Bridge pushed a hanging pine branch out of the way for Molly to pass, then he ducked under and walked beside her. "For me, it felt like my chest turned heavy and I wanted to cry. I felt lonely. Empty. Only inside my body, even though our bodies aren't empty because we have muscles and organs and veins and stuff. I'm describing it the only way I know how. Sometimes words aren't enough to explain feelings."

Molly stopped and peered up at him. "I didn't

cry, but my chest was heavy too. *Heavy* is a good word."

Here came the description from the Oxford Languages.

"Heavy means of great weight—difficult to lift or move. Of great density, thick or substantial. As an adjective, that is. There are other definitions if we used nouns or adverbs. But I don't think that applies here. I read that in the Oxford Languages."

Bridge hid his smile. Molly wouldn't understand the amusement. "You know a lot of words."

"I know all the words in Oxford Languages," she said matter-of-factly.

"All of them?"

"I don't lie."

Gunshots erupted again, and Bridge's heart stumbled. "Molly, crouch down. I don't know where those shots are coming from." Not close by though, so either Wendy hadn't shaken the sniper or he'd found her. Or she'd found him. He hoped the latter was the case. Tiny eyes reflected from a few feet away. Bears weren't commonly active at night, but that didn't mean they wouldn't run into one. These mountains were dangerous in more ways than a sniper.

The temperature was dropping and if they didn't find some kind of shelter or start a fire soon, it would become a brand-new danger for them. "You didn't happen to read a survival guide, did you?" he asked, half-joking and half-hopeful. The kid retained information like a hard drive.

"No."

"Let's move on. Walking will keep us warmer than sitting in the cold." Every few feet he switched on his flashlight for a little guidance, but he didn't want to run down the batteries. "What's in your backpack?"

"I don't know. It's not mine."

"Can I see it?"

"You can't see it?"

Literal. "Can I look inside it?"

"Yes." She shrugged out of the backpack as she continued to walk, being careful and using trees to help her.

Bridge unzipped the pack and shone the light inside. Food. Water bottles. Survival pack and batteries. Score! Wendy must have believed they might be stuck in the mountains for a stint of time. Actually, he had no idea what her plans were. They'd had little time to converse. He had batteries, which meant he could use his flashlight a little longer each time. Not too much though. If they were being tracked, it might as well be a lighthouse guiding a pirate ship to treasure.

Crunching and crackling of twigs and branches sent Bridge into high alert. He drew his gun.

"Molly," he whispered. "Hide behind that tree but don't run unless I tell you to. You understand?"

"I understand." Molly hurried behind the tree and Bridge slipped into the shadows.

Waiting.

Watching.

Wendy slunk through the mountain foliage, her side bruised and bloodied. Now she checked the tracker on her phone. She didn't need cell service to use it, which meant Bridge was six feet away and he'd probably heard her coming. "Bridge," she whispered. "It's me. Stand down."

He emerged like a looming shadow. "I heard shots again."

"I double-backed and followed the earlier shots. Found our shooter and ambushed him, but he put up a good fight." She winced and touched her side. "Took a knife and a few punches to the ribs, but I'll live. How's Molly?"

"She seems to be doing fine." He eyed her as she approached, then shined his flashlight on her face and flinched. "Jiminy Cricket," he murmured and touched her sore chin. "I'm sorry about that."

His earlier jab had bruised her, but she had endured far worse. Pointing to his side, then his arm where blood had seeped through his clothing, she said, "Yeah, well. Me too. You need stitches?"

"I don't know. I haven't had time to examine the damage. We've been on the move. I'm thinking you have some idea of where we're going? I have a lot of questions. What is going on? Why do you want Molly? Where are you taking her and to whom? And how did you know she was here?"

"Slow down, Tiger." She inwardly cringed, not meaning to use the nickname she'd given him. He bristled, but she pretended not to notice. "I can answer all your questions, but it's cold, and a blizzard is heading our way. We need to start a fire and rest awhile, then move ourselves off this mountain before it moves in midmorning."

"Won't they find us with a fir[\/
'e burning?"

"No. I've rendered the target useless."

Bridge nodded his understanding. "He's dead."

She sighed. "Not my first choice. I wanted information. But...it didn't go my way. Didn't really go his either." She never enjoyed taking a life and tried not to if she could maneuver around it but it had been kill or be killed back there. She'd had every intention of living.

"Let's find a place to start a fire. We can talk when Molly sleeps. I don't want her overhearing things she shouldn't. And she'll likely try to define everything we say. Literally."

Wendy smiled. She loved that about Molly. Even if her prior job as Molly's nanny had been an assignment, Wendy had loved spending time with the little girl. It had surprised Wendy how much she'd missed her when she arrived at the camp and saw Molly.

"There's a small clearing less than two clicks away. We can set up camp. I have pup tents and I don't think firewood will be difficult." She'd expected to walk Molly out of the camp and to the parking area but she'd planned for the possibility of a longer trek in the mountains. Her gut said it wasn't safe to double back and to continue with Plan B. Hadn't expected a blizzard blowing in though.

Once they reached the clearing, in mostly silence, Wendy set up camp while Bridge made a fire. Molly didn't say too much unless asked a direct question, but that was Molly's way. Two small tents easily popped up and she tucked a thermal blanket in each one to help them through the night. The temp had dropped sharply and she shivered even though she wore thermal gear under her clothing. Molly had scooted closer to the fire and was holding out her gloved hands. Her little face was windburned, but she'd been a real trooper.

Wendy opened up two cans of chicken noodle soup and cooked them in their cans over the fire, then rationed them into cups, giving Molly the lion's portion. "This will warm your belly and then you can sleep." She remembered the girl didn't like to be touched without permission. "Do you need anything else?"

"No. I'm fine, Nanny Wendy. Thank you."

"Nanny Wendy?" Bridge asked, his brow forming a deep divot.

"We'll talk later," she murmured and settled in next to Molly, who ate silently.

"Can I go to sleep now?" Molly asked after she finished the soup.

"Of course, hon."

Molly said good-night, then she crawled into her thermal blanket that zipped. Lighter than a regular sleeping bag, easier to tote around and just as warm. Wendy possessed only the two thermal blankets, and the extreme cold made it impossible for her or Bridge to spend the night without insulation. That was going to be a fun conversation later.

She stored the leftover cups and hung them away from the campsite to avoid attracting bears with the scent of food. She then rejoined Bridge at the fire, where he had added extra logs he had found. Molly was fast asleep inside her pup tent.

No one was left to buffer the conversation between them. She eased down by the fire, thankful for the blazing heat. The wind had strengthened and the inky sky spat flecks of snow.

"Tell me why you took Molly Wingbender," Bridge demanded, rubbing his hands together over the fire. "And why does she call you Nanny Wendy?"

"Why are *you* here at a horse camp in Tennessee?" she countered. If Bridge was here undercover, then the FBI expected a threat on the child. The question was, did they expect the threat to come from Wendy? Or had they finally figured out she hadn't killed Charlie Wingbender?

"Because the company I work for sent me here."

She frowned. "Is that what you call the Bureau these days?"

Bridge shivered and scooted closer to the fire. "I don't work for the Bureau. I resigned three Christmases ago."

When she'd left. Had he quit because of the damage she'd done?

"You had nothing to do with it," he said, as if reading her thoughts. "And I don't want to discuss why I did. It's personal. I work for Spears & Bow now. We provide protection all over the world. This is actually my first assignment."

Wendy never dreamed Bridge would leave the Bureau, but he had said that he too had planned to take a more 9–5 role once they'd married and started a family of their own. Same as she had said. Neither wanted to leave their jobs—at least at that time—and they had been okay with each other remaining in the field of justice. A lot had happened in three years. For them both.

"A botched kidnapping had David Wingbender calling Spears & Bow to keep extra protection on Molly. She arrived at the riders camp a week ago. They set me up as the horse guide and trainer. So imagine my surprise when Molly's taken again and this time by you. I'd ask if it was you trying to kidnap her the first time, but I know you don't botch missions, so…" He eyed her, waiting for an explanation.

If that were only true. Her last mission had been beyond botched and stolen three years of her life. "Have you heard of Mask?"

Bridge toggled his hand. "I know Charlie Wingbender was working on a project called Mask, but no details."

"It's a next-level deepfake technology. It will revolutionize the world in ways you can't imagine. Charlie was the designer. Once this project was complete, it was being sold to us—the American government. I was there undercover to make sure he finished it and remained safe. The best way in was as Molly's nanny. That's why she calls me Nanny Wendy."

"Your last mission," Bridge whispered. "It was this Mask mission involving the Wingbenders."

"Yes. The project was to be done by Christmas Eve morning and I was to arrive in Texas on the Spencer ranch…" To start their new life together. But he'd come home to a Dear John letter instead of her in person. She'd run underground. "Between the time I tucked Molly into bed and returned to Charlie's office—fifteen minutes tops—someone came in and murdered Charlie. When I got to him, he was dying. I knelt before him and he said to keep Molly safe and mouthed the word *liar*, which I wasn't sure what that meant."

"What happened?" Bridge laid another log on the fire. The sparks twirled in the air and fizzled out. Cracks and pops of wood echoed in the frosty night air, the snow spitting every now and again to warn that a greater, heavier snowfall would descend shortly.

"I called Anderson Crawley."

"Your supervisor at the CIA."

"Yes." Anderson had been a friend and handler at one time. About fifteen years her senior and completely gray, he had seen her through most of her missions. She'd trusted him. "He said to extract the research, the laptop and anything else pertinent and meet at a rendezvous point in San Jose. I'd be debriefed and pass off the research and then walk away. I was going to hop a plane from San Jose to Cedar Springs, Texas, and…" She trailed off. She hadn't done it exactly that way.

Bridge looked away. No doubt replaying that letter in his head. "You stayed undercover. To keep on with the bright, exciting career. I assume part of the research was missing. I hope you're happy with your choice to remain in the CIA. In the long run, I'm sure we're both happier."

Wendy had expected him to move on. It had been three years, but she felt the sting nonetheless. "I'm sure we are," she murmured. Should she tell him the whole truth? Would it be better to protect him by letting him believe a lie? No. No one was better off believing lies.

"After I called Anderson and told him the situation, I realized something. I heard a chopper in the background of the call, which isn't uncommon. We fly a lot of places but…there was also a chopper near Charlie's house at the same time. I went outside and there that bird was. Hovering just a few miles away."

Bridge cocked his head. "Are you saying that Anderson Crawley murdered Charlie?"

She nodded. "And burned me. I figured you'd

heard." Then she remembered he'd left the Bureau, though she wasn't sure of the circumstances. "You leaving…it wasn't because of my burn notice, was it?"

"No," he blurted. "I left, and I broke ties so I didn't hear you'd been burned."

When an asset or intelligence source was unreliable for one or many reasons, often fabrication, an official statement was issued to other agencies. No one could help her. Support her. She was a fugitive. Alone.

"According to Talia Dean, a tech analyst for the CIA who I worked with closely, photos surfaced of me over Charlie's lifeless body, with blood on my hands and my gun on the floor. It was incriminating. My best guess is, he tapped into the security footage and erased the truth but kept enough to frame me by using an early version of Charlie's Mask program. That early version had glitches and could be traced so he was reworking it when he was killed."

Bridge sat in silence, his eyes trained on the fire. Finally, he spoke. "Why didn't you reach out to me? Are you saying the letter you gave me was a lie?"

"I'm saying you couldn't protect me and the more you knew, the greater danger you were in. I had to clear my name. Wingbender never kept all his research together. He had pieces of coding stashed in flash drives all over the world. He had homes in twenty countries. Offices in dozens more. Ever since I was burned, I've been working on retrieving them all. I've found flash drives in Washington D.C., Omaha, Tampa, Montana, Budapest, Russia, South Korea, Nepal, Istanbul, Kenya and Japan. And I'm not the only one who has been hunting for them. Russia. North Korea. China. Iran. And Anderson."

"You've been up against them all? You never… I could have… I would have…" He balled a fist. "Do you have all the pieces of coding now?"

"No. And yes." Maybe she should have reached out to Bridge, but unlike her, he had family— family she dearly loved too—and ruthless criminals who wouldn't bat an eye before murdering them to keep Bridge in line. The only reason Wendy could come up with for why Anderson hadn't touched Bridge these past three years was because she had a few of the flash drives and he knew she'd destroy them if any harm came to Bridge or his family.

"What's that mean, Wendy? Lay it out straight. We have deadly people trying to take us out and abduct a child. I need all the information." His tone was tight and his nostrils flared. He had every right to be angry. Every right to hate her.

"I found the last the piece of code."

"Where?"

"Here. It's not a flash drive. It's a person."

Molly.

THREE

Bridge's mouth hung open like a largemouth bass. "Molly? How?"

"If you've spent half a second with the child, then you know she has a photographic memory. If she reads it, she memorizes it. Some people have to absorb the information and understand it, then they never forget it. But not Molly. Molly only has to see something to know it."

Bridge added another log to the fire, shivering from the cold, but he had to know more. "Her father had her study the code, then he deleted it?" He would have had to have realized that would put a huge target on his daughter's fragile back. Why would anyone do that? Especially a father.

"I don't know if he deleted it. But in three years I haven't found it and neither has anyone else. So I'm thinking she's it. No one would suspect, except me, because I actually spent time with her as a nanny. And the other thing is if you tell her not to tell, she won't. Molly doesn't break rules. She follows them to the letter."

He had experienced that as well. "So you came to extract her. Why?"

"I need her to translate the code, which would help prove that the footage of me killing Charlie was a fake—set up through an earlier version of the Mask software. But it won't help me prove Anderson killed Charlie. I didn't witness his murder and the footage was wiped—other than what incriminates me. I also can't prove what I suspect—that Anderson had planned to double-cross his country and sell the Mask technology to an enemy nation. I should have a game plan, but I don't. I can't be sure how many agencies might be involved, and now that I'm burned… none of them will believe or help me."

He believed her. Wendy would kill no one in cold blood. Sure, her job required taking out bad people sometimes, like the guy trying to murder her in the woods, but she would never turn like that. Never betray her country. If she said she was innocent, then she was.

"So how do we find proof that Anderson Crawley burned you because he knows you have his number? Whatever we have to do, I'm in."

"I'm not sure. The only person I trust in the agency is Talia. And I try not to ask too much from her because she needs this job and I don't want to put her in danger. She's hacked into Anderson's Agency computer but found nothing. She hasn't been able to retrieve his personal laptop."

"In three years, you haven't broken into his home and done it yourself?" That seemed like the first item of business to take on.

"I did." She smirked. "But he locks it up when he's not on it. Which tells me it has valuable information. And I tried to crack the code to the safe, but he changes it regularly and unpredictably. Before you ask why I didn't steal the whole safe, it's built into the wall and wired separately from his security system."

And Wendy didn't have time to surveil Anderson long enough to figure out the code, he realized. She'd been running all over the world retrieving pieces of coding. Alone.

Wendy had no family. Her parents died when she was in junior high, and her grandmother passed when she turned nineteen. But on the run she was truly alone. He felt the crack in his chest but refused to acknowledge it. "So, what's your immediate plan?"

"My immediate plan was to collect Molly and take her to a safe house of mine." Most operatives had safe places they told no one about in case things went sideways. And it often did. Being a spy wasn't exactly a predictable job.

"Where is this safe house?"

"The closest one is in Bear Valley. Ten miles from the bottom of this mountain."

"That's doable."

"Yeah, but I didn't expect to be hung out by the baddies. I don't know how they found me other than they had eyes on Molly. Have you noticed anyone lurking? Had any gut feelings?" She pulled her heavy down jacket tighter against her slender frame.

"No. I mean, I've been on high alert from the start but… I don't know. Today felt weird. Like a foreboding deep in my bones. The only people privy to Molly's location are my team, Molly's uncle and a couple directors at the horse camp that needed to be informed."

Wendy drew up her knees and wrapped her arms around them. "Money talks. You know this. Someone at the camp had to have been approached, or maybe David told someone he thought he could trust. We need to contact him once we have cell service. Or you need to. I don't want anyone to know I'm with you. It's dangerous. In fact, you need to give me Molly and leave camp. I can keep her safe. No point dragging you into this."

Because she didn't want to be near him? Was it hard on her? Or was her heart so hard she simply saw him as baggage? Dead weight. A thorn in her side.

"I've been hired to do a job, Wendy. I'm not resigning."

Wendy cocked her head, long blond hair falling around her shoulders. "Speaking of resigning. Why did you leave the Bureau?" She was persistent. He'd give her that. "Was it because of me?"

"Not everything is about you, Wendy."

"I didn't mean it that way, Bridge."

He knew. He was being a jerk. "I know. Sorry. It wasn't that."

"Was it over an undercover case you were working?" she murmured.

"Yeah. But I'm not up for talking about it, like I said earlier. We need to trek out of here at first light. You have a car nearby?"

"Outside the camp. But it's the CIA, which means it's been checked, compromised and eyes are on it, waiting for me. We need to hike off the mountain and rent a car in town. Meanwhile, let's take a look at the cuts and see if they need to be stitched. Then we need to try to sleep."

He hauled up his coat and lifted his shirt where she'd sliced his side with the blade. He growled when he saw how deep the cut was. "I probably need a couple."

Wendy retrieved a first-aid kit and a needle and thread. "You shine the light and I'll handle it."

"Well, you owe me that at least, since you inflicted it."

He frowned, and she grinned. "You know I'm good with a blade." She removed her gloves.

He rolled his eyes as she swiped an alcohol wipe across his side. He winced at the sting.

"Sorry," she muttered. Her fingers were warm against his cool skin. She met his gaze. "You, uh…you been working out harder than last time I saw you."

"Yeah. I've had some spare time."

"It looks… You look good."

He wished she'd shut up. He didn't want to hear her compliment him. And her pupils had dilated. Well, it was clear that she was still attracted to him. But he didn't want that either.

"Get it done," he said in a clipped tone.

"Okay." She didn't bother to tell him to take a deep breath before the point of the needle entered his tender flesh. He ground his teeth, clenching his jaw, and she ran the needle in and out of his skin until she'd stitched up the wound. "Right as rain."

He lowered his shirt and caught her staring again.

He then checked his upper arm where she'd made another cut. It didn't need a stitch. But nei-

hind him drew his attention, but he kept his eyes focused on what crept in the night.

"You heard that?" he whispered. He didn't figure she'd allow herself to fall into a deep slumber.

"Yeah. You think it might be a bear or deer?"

"Could be."

"I'm going to go check it out. I'll loop around and come in from behind it." She secured a backpack and drew her weapon. "I have bear spray too. If you hear me whistle, you'll know it's an animal."

"I can go and you can stay here."

"Don't go all alpha male, Bridge. It doesn't become you." She slipped into the shadows, becoming one herself. Bridge positioned himself in front of Molly's tent. No matter what, they had to keep her safe.

Another snap came from about fifty feet away. But he heard nothing from the direction Wendy had slinked off in.

Please be a bear. A bear they could put down or run off—hopefully. An assassin was a different animal and deadlier.

The air stilled. Silence hung.

Then a shot rang out. One, then another.

His only thought was Wendy.

Wendy jumped from the top of the tree branch where she'd climbed and dropped on the sniper.

A new sniper, which meant whoever was in the woods wasn't alone. Or...more than one person was after her and Molly, which ramped up the challenge of escaping this mountain and getting to her safe house in Bear Valley. She might have to take Molly farther, like her place in Florida. For now, she had to deal with this threat.

The gun fired as she landed on top of the assailant, knocking him for a loop with the surprise attack. She struck the neck adjacent to his Adam's apple, nailing the vagus nerve just right, and he went night-night. She pilfered through his heavy military green coat, finding another handgun and bullets. After shoving them in her own backpack, she searched for anything else. Two knives and a grenade. A grenade. Nice. She pocketed that too and finished stripping him of all weaponry. He had no wallet. She wasn't surprised to find no identification. She carried none either.

Pulling the thin rope from her pocket, she secured him to the tree. Training said to render him useless. He was the enemy and would come at them again. But she wasn't in a fight to the death, until she was forced to be. She'd incapacitated him and that was enough. Maybe these past three years had made her soft. She wouldn't have hesitated then. But now things were different. If the would-be assassin was any good, he'd eventually free himself from her binds and they'd be long gone. If not… She refused to think of that.

Once he was secured to the tree, she slapped his face to wake him, but brittle wood cracking and leaves crunching told her this guy wasn't alone. How many were there? And who had dispatched them? She lifted his ski mask and shined a light on his face. If she had to guess, she'd say he was of Russian descent, but that didn't necessarily make him Russian. She hadn't been able to determine nationality of the other man she'd taken out.

She darted into the shadows awaiting whoever was trekking through the mountain, hunting her and Molly—now Bridge too. The movement silenced suddenly. Had the predator sniffed out another predator hovering nearby? She waited as the snow grew heavier. A thin layer now covered the ground and revealed her position. Biting down on her frustration, she moved to the next tree. No light. But the snow was bright enough for a good tracker to pick up on her destination. And no one would send amateurs after Wendy unless they were idiots. Or underestimated her.

Gunfire rang out from the direction she'd just come from.

Molly! Bridge!

Wendy bolted and raced back to camp but via

another route in case whoever was tracking her assumed that would be her position. Another shot fired, then a succession of rounds. Her heart thundered like a violent storm in her chest as she pushed harder to return and rescue them. She trusted Bridge to do his job. He was an excellent marksman and skilled in fighting. Tough as any man she'd ever known. But she had no idea who was after her and what their level of training might be.

And then she had to remember North Korea was after the codes. She could not let them capture Molly or Bridge like they'd captured her last year when she'd been searching for the missing flash drives in Tokyo. The pain. The torture. It hit her gag reflex and pumped a fresh round of adrenaline through her.

She didn't want to think about that stint. Six months. In darkness. Not a stitch of light. Only pain. Terror. Until she finally escaped. Thank God! But the scars—inside and out—would always remain. If they got ahold of Bridge and Molly… She didn't want to think about that.

The pup tents appeared, but the camp was empty, save for a low burning fire. The thermal blankets and supplies were gone. As she surveyed the camp, a force smacked into her and toppled her to the ground and a man the size of the Hulk reared his boulder of a fist back. She jerked her head to the side, escaping his obliteration of her face.

With a hint of cinnamon on his breath, he strung a few expletives, then he gripped her jacket collar, pulled her up and slammed her head against the ground. Pain reverberated through her system. Much more of this brutality and she'd be the dog losing this fight. When he raised her up again, she pushed forward, gaining momentum and headbutted his masked face. He released her, and she shot her hand up and connected with his nose. The crunch echoed in the silent night, and he howled and tossed a few more expletives.

She'd broken it. Now to break the rest of him. Snagging her knife from her coat pocket, she flicked it open and slashed it across his abdomen. Not enough to kill him. Wendy needed answers. She also knew it was going to take a lot more pain to make him talk, but she'd been trained and was skilled in making men talk. Even Hulks. Every human being had a breaking point. She only had to find it, which meant pressing and pushing until the weak area was exposed and then she would have him.

He grabbed his stomach, and she slashed his right cheek, then his left. "Not going to be your day, big boy."

Fury flickered in his dark eyes and the beast

within awakened and rushed her like a bull with a burr under his saddle. Bucking and thrashing, he charged her, but she had speed going for her against his strength.

She retrieved a second knife from her waistband. Knives were more personal as they required moving into one's space to wield them. Up close. She spun them in her hands like Doc Holliday with his gun and grounded herself, prepared for him to make another move.

"I'm going to kill you with my bare hands and enjoy it!" He sneered and stormed her. She swiped the knife, but he dodged it. All she had to do was avoid his bare hands. If he got a good grip or a punch, she'd be toast.

"Who are you working for? Russia? Us?"

He didn't answer.

"I'm going to force it out of you," Wendy said. "Those cuts were just a prelude. You don't want more of what I have to give."

Heedless of her warning, he rushed her. She darted to the side and pivoted, running her blade through his side and ignoring his howl of pain. This time, she'd gone deeper. Made her point extremely clear.

"I can let you live," she said, "or I can put you in the grave."

"I can bring pain too," her attacker spat out.

"You don't scare me." But she was scared.

This was also her job. The only thing she knew how to do.

Gripping her knives, she raised them. He was here to do one thing. Kill her. Or take her and torture her until she gave up the flash drives. Surviving six months in a North Korea prison was no holiday for her. She could endure this guy.

He deked right and pivoted left, catching her off guard and knocking her to the ground. She lost one knife upon the jarring impact. He wrapped his monstrous hand around her throat and squeezed so hard she thought he'd crush her hyoid bone. With his other hand, he grabbed her armed hand and slammed it onto the ground until she dropped the knife.

No weapon in hand.

And she was being strangled by King Kong. She wasn't stupid enough to believe she could overpower him. But she knew he didn't want her dead. He would like her passed out. Passed out gave him the opportunity to take her. Nope. She couldn't let him do that.

Summoning her training, she shoved her fingers into his eyes and he yelped and tightened his hold on her neck. Her lungs constricted and her eyes began to bulge and burn. She was losing strength. Losing vision. Spots broke into her clear line of vision and she knew it would be seconds before she lost consciousness.

A gunshot rang out.

Hulk wailed and grabbed his left shoulder, releasing her neck. She gasped in air as another shot fired, and he dropped, his full weight collapsing on top of her. He had to weigh two-eighty, maybe more. His crushing pounds forced air from her lungs and she let out a grunt, then checked his pulse.

Dead.

"Wendy!"

Bridge. She'd never been more thankful to hear that voice. He raced over and knelt beside her, scanning the woods.

Somehow she found the breath to ask, "Where's Molly?"

"Safe." Bridge kicked the beast off her and ripped off his mask. "You know him?"

"I don't know him. Or the other guy. I tied him to a tree."

"Going soft?" he asked and pilfered the man's pockets, retrieving weapons and shoving them in his waistband and backpack.

"I don't know. He's without hands in a snowstorm and vulnerable to animals. I might have showed more mercy by making it quick." She stood and sighed. "I never enjoy taking a life."

"Wendy, he was out to kill you. I did what I had to and so did you. Let's survive and keep going."

"Thank you."

He nodded. "Follow me." Bridge forged ahead and Wendy brought up the rear. Even if she wanted to speak, her throat throbbed and her head ached. She needed the silence. A click away, Bridge pointed to a dead tree that had fallen. "Molly, it's me. You can come out."

Molly popped up from inside the tree. Leaves had stuck to strands of hair hanging around her shoulders. "That tree smelled bad. I do not aspire to be in any more trees."

"I'm not going to make that promise," Bridge said.

Smart call. If they told Molly it would never happen again and it did, she'd have a meltdown.

"Are you hurt, Nanny Wendy?" Molly asked.

"I'm okay."

"Okay means satisfactory but not exceptionally or especially good. I read that in the Oxford Languages. You're not especially good?"

"No. No, I'm not especially or exceptionally good. I'm just satisfactory right now." She smiled at the child.

"Are we going back to our tents?" Molly asked.

Wendy's eyes met Bridge's, and it surprised her how after three years they could still communicate without speaking a word. Going back to their campsite was dangerous. They had no clue how many men were on this mountain and one of them might untie himself. Maybe she should have rendered him useless.

Snowflakes dotted her lashes, and she blinked several times. They needed shelter. Warmth. Needed to escape the elements. "Shine that light over here, Bridge." She pulled out a satellite map she'd printed of the mountain before coming here. She found their location and scanned the area. "About eight miles east is a campground. We might find an abandoned cabin to hole up in until morning or until the storm passes. Either way, we need shelter as soon as possible."

"Agreed." Bridge turned to Molly. "You up for a little hike?"

"Eight miles is not little. Little means small in size, amount or degree. I read that—"

"In the Oxford Languages," Bridge said. "We know."

Wendy caught his eye and raised an eyebrow.

"Sorry, Molly. I'm frustrated is all."

"It's *okay*." Molly raised her chin and Bridge chuckled. Molly had a made a little joke. She normally never used humor, nor did she seem to pick up on it. But she'd made it clear she wasn't especially good.

Wendy pointed east. "Let's go. Time isn't on our side."

"Time isn't on anyone's side. It's not a person,"

Molly commented, following behind Wendy as Bridge brought up the rear.

"You're right." Wendy was too tired to explain it right now. She prayed they'd find a cabin or some kind of shelter and make it the eight miles without incident, but her prayers were cut short when she heard the distinct and terrifying noise.

The high-pitched roar resounded from the left, and Wendy cautiously pivoted as glowing eyes locked in on them from the branch above.

Mountain lion!

FOUR

The mountain lion lowered its head in a stalking stance. Bridge put his arm out and pushed Molly behind him. "Let's back away slowly and maybe it'll let us go." He didn't want to injure or kill the magnificent beast but he had to protect them. "Why don't you take Molly and I'll be right behind."

The mountain lion let out a deafening roar and bared its very large, very long fangs. Bridge hollered. "Scat cat! Scat!" He clapped his hands hoping the noise and yelling would scare it away, but the animal stood its ground. It was thin— too thin—which meant it was hungry. Mountain lions didn't usually prey on people but hungry animals acted in desperation and he wasn't chancing it.

It crept toward him and he backed away. From the crunching and snapping of twigs, branches and leaves behind him, he knew Wendy and

Molly were moving away from him and the mountain lion. Good.

The paws on this thing were as big as Bridge's face. And the claws were razor sharp, ready to shred him like cheese on a metal grater.

It roared again and Bridge knelt, grabbing a thick limb that had fallen. "Easy, fella," he said, gripping the limb in his hand as he continued backing away. He couldn't turn his back on it nor could he run. That was like throwing a yarn ball in front of a cat.

He waved the branch and hollered, "Get! Get!"

When that didn't work, he reluctantly drew his Glock. He only had thirteen rounds and no extra bullets. Firing a warning shot meant one less bullet to protect them from whoever was trying to kill Wendy and kidnap Molly. The question was, did they know Molly was the missing piece of code to the Mask software or, a darker thought, did someone know Wendy had a soft spot for the kid and used Molly to draw out Wendy and steal the pieces of code she'd spent the past few years searching for? Either way, he had to keep Wendy and the child safe.

The mountain lion went into attack position and Bridge breathed a prayer and then fired the gun over the mountain lion's head, bark raining down. The mountain lion sprinted into the woods and Bridge headed the other direction.

About fifty feet away he heard movement. He low whistled, like a bird, and waited.

No return signal from Wendy or a holler. Had she taken the kid and ditched him? She was good at vanishing into thin air. Hairs prickled on his neck and as he turned someone rushed him from the cluster of trees on the north side.

Bridge lowered his body as the attacker made contact, flipping him over his head onto the hard ground as snow fell on the mountain.

They weren't getting off this mountain tonight.

Maybe not at all.

How many killers had been sicced on them and by whom?

A man dressed in a camouflage ghillie suit, which clued in Bridge he was former military, sprang to his feet with skill and power. Bridge was about to be in a real fight with a formidable foe.

He needed the man alive for questioning. Was he one of Wendy's old handler's errand boys or was he working for someone else?

"Where is she?" the man asked in a deep gritty voice. "We don't want you. We want the woman. You tell me and I let you live."

"You underestimate me, pal."

Ghillie Suit Guy drew a bowie knife. "Then

it's going to become painful for you, *pal*," he remarked.

He charged Bridge and he dodged, but the guy was like lightning and attacked again. Bridge sucked in his gut and barely escaped the blade. Sweat trickled down his temples and spine as they danced this way a few more seconds, then when the attacker lunged again, Bridge caught his wrist and slammed him against a tree. The assassin hit his head against the trunk and Bridge beat his arm against the tree until he dropped the blade.

He kicked it away and slammed him once again against the hard wood, but the guy brought up a fist and clipped his chin. The sharp pain reached his brain and reverberated throughout his bones. He had a good swing.

Pushing off the tree, he rushed Bridge, knocking him to the ground. He landed on a fallen limb and his back screamed in pain. A large stone from a nearby creek lay next to him and he grabbed it, bringing it up with all the force he could muster, and cracked it against the side of the man's face.

He crumpled to the ground and Bridge quickly patted him down and found nylon rope shoved into one of his ghillie suit pockets. He dragged him to the tree and made quick work to tie him securely.

This man was going to tell him what he needed to know.

Or he was going to feel the pain.

Once he had him tied, he checked the guy's pulse, then slapped his face to snag his attention and wake him. It worked.

The man struggled to free himself but this wasn't Bridge's first interrogation. "No use fighting, but I understand the need to try. I'm a civilized man so I'm going to ask you a few questions and if you answer them, and I believe you, I'll make sure you don't die on the mountain."

The attacker didn't speak. Chances were he was former black ops and wouldn't talk. He'd die first. Bridge was going to take a crack though. "What do you want with the asset?" He avoided using Wendy's name. This guy might have instructions but no real insight or information. "What's your assignment? Take her or render her useless?"

Nothing.

Snow fell in big flat flakes and the temperature continued to drop. This man had to know he'd never survive the night tied to a tree. "Blizzard's coming. You do the math. You aren't here on a government job. Your asset was burned. So if you think you're serving your country, you're being lied to. And if you're simply attempting a payday, you won't be alive to receive a dime. You and I both know this. So what's it going to be? Talk to me and live or die in silence."

Nothing.

Fine. Bridge didn't want to walk away but the guy was giving him no choice. He turned and started into the darkness when the man finally spoke.

"Okay. I'll talk but don't leave me here. I received a message on a dark website. Asset was a woman. A photo of her and a kid. I was to bring the woman in alive. She has something the employer wants but I have no idea what. I just know that whoever brings her in alive to the rendezvous point receives four point two million dollars in an offshore account."

"Where is the rendezvous point?"

"I don't know. We have to show proof of life through a video and then the destination will be given."

Bridge growled under his breath. "Was this a personal message or a bulletin?"

"Bulletin."

Great. That meant anyone could have seen the public ad to bring in Wendy and the mountain location given to find her. There could be dozens of people on this mountain attempting her abduction, and when Wendy fought back, they'd have no choice but to kill her to stay alive. They might lose their money, but when their lives were on the line, it would be a fight to the death.

Now he had to protect her from some phantom who wanted her brought in. Anderson probably, but it could be anyone who wanted the pieces of code she'd been collecting since she'd been gone. He'd have to help her off the mountain, to a safe house, find who was behind this and bring them to justice, and keep Molly alive too. David, her uncle, would be beside himself when he found out she'd been compromised when Wendy attempted to take Molly.

He couldn't leave this man to die and he couldn't cut him loose either. He'd keep trying to find Wendy. What was he supposed to do? He prayed for wisdom and decided to untie his hands. "You get one shot at mercy, dude. The asset you've been hunting isn't as merciful. Remember that."

Bridge didn't wait for a reply and ran into the darkness, hoping Wendy hadn't made off with Molly, leaving Bridge in the wind. They needed each other.

He low-whistled and waited for a response. But the mountain was eerily silent as animals sought shelter from the snowstorm. The snow was accumulating. Not quite two inches but it was falling faster and harder. They needed shelter and quickly. He whistled again and about twenty clicks south, he heard a return whistle. Wendy hadn't left him behind again. He was relieved and a little surprised.

He followed the whistle and gave out another. When it was once again returned, he made his way into a heavy thicket of bramble, trees and bushes. Wendy was huddled with Molly who was shivering.

"Well?" she asked him.

"I showed some mercy."

"You're going soft," she muttered but smiled. She stood. "We have to find shelter or create one. It's getting colder and we can't leave the mountain until first light."

Bridge worried they wouldn't make it off at all if the temps kept plummeting and the snow didn't let up. But he refrained from sharing that information for fear Molly would panic. Though, aside from shivering, she appeared super chill. They needed a fire but the smoke and light would be a beacon calling out all assassins. Although with the snow falling so fast and hard, it might mask the smoke.

Wendy hauled her backpack on. "Can you hike a little longer, Molly?"

"Yes. But I'm cold and hungry."

Bridge was too.

Molly nodded and hitched her backpack up. Bridge pulled Wendy aside and kept his voice low. "You've been advertised on the dark web. Four point two million dollars to be brought to a rendezvous point upon proof-of-life video. We need to find a place where we can communicate with my team and have them hack into the dark web and this site, retrieve a location or a name."

Wendy laughed. "Yeah, because someone this sophisticated hasn't already routed it to ping off a million different towers. It's the dark web for a reason, Bridge."

She was right but her cynicism was new. Wendy had always been positive, though her job saw the underbelly of powerful people and governments. What happened the past few years to steal her positive outlook? And why did he care? She hadn't trusted him enough to ask for help back then. He could have. Would have. Even if he'd been in a dark place after losing a child and a colleague. She was his bright spot. Instead, he'd returned home to even more darkness. She no longer had a place in his heart. He was going to help see her off the mountain, then he was taking Molly and bring her safely to David. Bridge wouldn't lose another child on his watch. He couldn't.

Wendy tried to keep her fear in check. She didn't want Bridge to know she'd lost some of her mojo since being taken hostage and tortured in North Korea. The only thing that had gotten her through was remembering how Paul and Silas in the Bible sang praises in prison at midnight and the doors to the jail cells opened. They stayed in but when she had the chance to run, she'd taken it.

Now all she wanted was to clear her name and walk away from it all. But what was her next move? All she'd ever known was work for the CIA. She had no other skills. Hers was a particular set that reminded her of Liam Neeson in all those *Taken* movies. Now wasn't the time to ruminate on her future. If she didn't get her head in the game and focus, she might not have a future.

Anderson had no doubt put the extraction notice out on her. He wanted her alive so he could retrieve the pieces of coding for the Mask program. He didn't even care whom he sold it to. He only wanted the money. How long had he been corrupted? When did it happen for him? After Elizabeth died? His wife had had cystic fibrosis and needed special care around the clock. Good and private medical care was hard to come by. She suspected he started his downhill spiral as a way to keep his wife comfortable and cared for.

Selling out was wrong for any reason but she understood wanting to move heaven and earth for the person you loved most. Wendy would have taken a bullet for Bridge. He'd been her everything. Her rock and her soft place to land. She loved his gentle heart and his hard head. If things had turned out differently, she'd be married to him with children of their own right now. Well, one baby, although twins ran in his family—a family she had loved dearly and been a part of without question. His youngest siblings, Rhode and Sissy, were fraternal twins.

Snapping fingers caught her attention and pulled her back to reality. "Hey," Bridge said, "where'd you go?"

"Nowhere." Nowhere he needed to be privy to. "We need to make a shelter of some kind and we need to move fast. It's freezing and we all know what that means."

Molly spoke for the first time in a while. She was probably afraid too. Poor kid. "We could end up with hypothermia. Hypothermia is the condition of having an abnormally low body temperature, typically one that is dangerously low. I read that in the Oxford Languages online."

Of course she did. She had the entire thing memorized. That's how her brilliant mind worked. Wendy couldn't imagine having that kind of gift. And she couldn't imagine her own father using it for a piece of weaponry the world wanted. Why would he do such a thing? Bridge had wondered the same thing earlier. "Well, if we make a shelter, we can start a fire and warm up." She pulled an axe from her backpack.

Bridge laughed. "You're toting a Mary Poppins bag. You have a lampstand in there too?"

Wendy grinned. She'd always loved Bridge's sarcastic and occasionally dry humor.

"Mary Poppins," Molly said, "is a fictional character. Nanny Wendy couldn't possibly have her bag and a lampstand can't fit in a backpack."

"You're right," Bridge said. "What was I thinking?"

Bridge took the ax from Wendy. "I'll start cutting evergreen branches and you secure us some kindling."

She saluted. "Molly, can you help me collect branches and twigs for firewood?"

Molly nodded and they began foraging for kindling.

"Don't leave my eyeline, okay? I want to make sure I can see you at all times. Keep you safe."

"Okay."

The pine trees had lost several limbs from the wind and weight of the snow. Working to collect them helped to keep up her body temperature but every pop and crack had her on high alert. She was being hunted, stalked and not by one person but anyone who wanted 4.2 million dollars. That was a lot of incentive. They had to bring her in alive, but she wasn't going anywhere, which meant an extraction might turn into an execution.

Wendy's number one priority was Molly's safety though. She wasn't sure how this nightmare was affecting the child since Molly didn't seem to be scared of things that might normally frighten a child. She was logical about everything. But Wendy would do her best to keep her as free from trauma as she possibly could. The child had already lost so much. So many people she loved. And been sent to a camp to be safe.

How did the bad guys figure out where she was? They must have had a phantom on her. Wendy had never done phantom work. She was good at making herself disappear but a phantom was something else entirely and required a skill set she didn't possess. Phantoms were agents who could hide in plain sight, right under their own family's nose and never be detected. They were often educated in dozens of languages and makeup artist techniques. They were like magicians without the rabbits. Able to create illusions in their appearance and disappearances.

She only knew one phantom personally but he was off the grid. Hadn't been seen or heard from in years. For all she knew the phantom could be masquerading as Bridge. They were that good at disguise and even voice modification.

If one of these people was sent to keep an eye

on David Wingbender and Molly, then he could have even been at the camp or anywhere on the Wingbender property at any time. With those skills plus regular operative training, phantoms were deadly, striking before one would even know they'd been struck.

A phantom had to be around to know Molly had been sent to the camp. For all she knew, the house had been bugged. David wasn't like his brother, Charlie. Tech savvy he was not. His work was in the entertainment industry as an intellectual property attorney. The only bugs he understood was Bunny. But he did have financial advisors and board members to the Wingbender fortune who were savvy and could have easily been bought and working with or for Anderson. That man was some kind of persuasive.

Wendy shivered as a gale blew through the trees, snow riding the wind and falling in clumps. Molly stood with an arm full of branches. "Is this enough?" she asked.

"Great job, Moll."

"It's Molly. Molly Wingbender. I don't use nicknames."

Right. She'd forgotten. She didn't have Molly's memory. "Sorry. Let's take them back to Bridge and help him make a shelter." As they double backed to the space they were setting up camp, the wind howled and twigs snapped and creaked. She paused and stopped Molly with a halt sign. Then she put her fingers to her mouth to signal Molly to stay quiet so she could listen.

Critters or creepers? She wasn't sure.

The forest went silent. Only soft rustling in the branches above them. But anyone could be camouflaged and sitting up in the trees, watching and waiting. A chill ran down her spine and she motioned Molly to move on ahead. Wendy couldn't see anyone, but she felt them lurking. Waiting for the right moment to spring into action and try to trap her.

"Stay close, Molly. We're not safe out—" Wendy shrieked as she stepped on something hard and suddenly she was bound in thick ropes and sailing through the air. She'd been caught in a literal trap and was now hanging above the trees. "Run, Molly! Find Bridge. Drop the branches and run. Now!"

FIVE

Molly dropped the branches as instructed and bolted. Wendy prayed the child would be safe and make it in time. Right now, she had to worry about this trap and how she hadn't seen it. It was done well. Completely secure. Had this trap been out here for a long time? Or had someone set it recently for her, covering it with branches and then the snow filled in the gaps?

If it was the latter, then she was in real trouble. She managed to pull her boot knife out and begin sawing to cut herself free but the ropes were thick. It wouldn't be a quick slice.

And she had little to no time before a would-be captor might find her.

Crunching and cracking on snow and forest debris sounded. Too big to be a critter. Could be a bear or a mountain lion or even a wolf. Or worse—someone who wanted a lot of money and was willing to risk it all for a payday. Wendy continued to keep her wits even if her heart was sprinting along her ribs. She sawed until the rope gave and she braced herself as she fell the fifteen feet to the ground. Even with the snow and pine needles the impact was jarring and she felt it clear to her head. Now she was on the cold snowy ground with a heavy web of rope holding her captive, and in the distance, a shadow emerged from the tree line. She worked the knife to loosen the knot that would open the top of the rope trap. Time wasn't on her side but she worked furiously, sweat slicking down her back and temples.

Come on, Wendy. Move. Slow is smooth and smooth is fast. She repeated the mantra over and over as the big shadowy figure, like bigfoot, approached at a calm and steady pace. *See, Wen, he knows smooth is fast.*

She wasn't going to make it in time. She put her knife between her teeth and pulled her Glock, firing a shot. The figure darted into the woods and she crouched, hoping he wouldn't return fire. The dark-web bulletin specified alive but said nothing of wounds and maiming. All he had to do was fire into her leg, staunch the bleeding but render her incapacitated. She finally cut through and the rope opened, falling at her sides. Finagling out of it, she darted into the woods and away from their campsite. She couldn't lead them to Molly or Bridge. Bridge could hold his own but Molly was just an innocent child.

She reminded herself she wasn't just running from one person. Others were also out here. Maybe even teams working together to split the pie. As far as Wendy was concerned, danger was on every side of her, closing in and ready to win. She raced through the trees, leading the assailant farther south. Footfalls sounded behind her. He hadn't given up. He might even be wearing night-vision goggles, which put him at an advantage.

She ducked behind a huge tree and kept her back flush against it, catching her breath and listening to see where her enemy might be. The forest became quiet. No footfalls. No crunching. Cracking or snapping.

Just the wind, branches creaking and her own breath misting out in front of her like fog. Her lungs burned and she worked to slow her heartrate in order to regulate her breathing. She waited and when she'd given it five or six minutes, she slowly knelt and picked up a pine cone. Time to test if the coast was clear. She tossed the pine cone at a tree about six feet away and a bullet fired into it, spraying bits and bark. Wendy hadn't lost her tracker and wasn't free from danger yet.

But sitting here wasn't going to keep her safe.

She darted in the opposite direction she'd thrown the pine cone and ran into the darkness. Only the white snow gave off a dim light. She used it to her advantage and forged ahead.

Wendy spotted a hollowed-out log. Without another thought, she jumped inside and shrank down as footsteps approached. She gripped her gun and waited. But the footsteps passed right by her and continued on. Waiting until they were no longer in hearing distance, she rose from the spongey tree trunk and circled back the way she came, collecting the firewood and returning to camp.

She released a breath when she saw Molly stacking the wood.

"Bridge isn't back yet," Molly said. "But I did what you asked. Now what do I do?"

Wendy wanted to hug the child but she didn't care for physical touch and that was even if you asked permission. "I'm glad you're safe. Let's make a clearing—" She stopped when she heard footsteps behind her. "Get behind me, Molly," Wendy said and raised her gun.

But it was Bridge approaching and she sighed in relief.

"You okay?" he asked, dropping more branches on an already big pile.

"Little trouble but we're okay for now." Wendy would keep an eye out for the attacker in case he too double backed and found them. At least she knew he was out there, and if he approached again, she wouldn't be able to be as merciful.

She went to work helping Bridge layer logs and limbs to make a small square shape, then they draped branches over it to help keep out the wind. Then she found some moss and shoved it in between cracks. It was pitiful and probably not something they could use for long but it was better than being in the elements without any covering.

Once inside they used their hands to dig a hole and placed a few sticks in it. Bridge made an opening in the roof. "It might be too smoky in here without a chimney but we don't have time for that, and I don't know if the snow will conceal the smoke well enough or not right now. We could keep going, but I don't know how much Molly has left in her without resting."

"I agree. We can crawl into our thermal blanket sleeping bags and huddle. Best we can do. Worst-case we build a fire outside or... I don't know. I'm so tired." Wendy yawned and helped Molly into her blanket.

Then she rolled out her own. "You up for sharing?" Molly wouldn't have allowed either of them to share hers. She had a thing about personal space.

Bridge massaged the nape of his neck. "Uh... sure."

Obviously he wasn't too keen on getting all up in her personal space. Neither was she. It had been three years since she'd even seen him. The closest contact they'd had since seeing one another again was to kick the snot out of each other over Molly. Not the same as climbing into a cocoon together.

He slipped into the thermal blanket next to her. Wendy inhaled a scent that was all Bridge. Masculine and enticing with a hint of fresh scent deodorant mingling with pine and other earthy smells that now clung to him. Wendy's stomach jittered as his leg pressed against hers, but she zipped up the bag, smooshing them together like sardines in a can—but with better smells.

Bridge skittered to his side for room. His frame was far bulkier than the last time she'd seen him. What would he think of her? She'd lost weight and muscle in the past three years. Not that she was weak, but being on the run hadn't afforded her the normal routine to work out, and then captivity hadn't helped.

The sense of confinement needled into her chest, tightening it.

"You okay?" he whispered and she caught cinnamon on his breath. He'd always loved cinnamon breath mints. Never was without them.

"Just a little claustrophobic." Might as well be honest.

"Since when?"

Bridge's face was mere inches away from hers, close enough to see the faint lines crinkling the outer edges of his eyes. He was aging well and she liked the beard. The thermal blanket had done its job, warming them up using their body heat, but now she was too warm and her insides felt feverish. "I guess in the past three years. I'm not the woman I used to be."

Captivity will do that to a person. Harden them. Create fears that they never had before. Incite paranoia. To name a few.

"I'm not the man I used to be either," he confessed. Did his reason for leaving the FBI have something to do with it? He'd made it clear, twice, that conversation wasn't on the table for discussion. Wendy had no choice but to respect his privacy.

"I'm not going to be able to sleep. Too keyed up," she said. "If you want to doze, I'll take first watch. I just needed to warm up."

His hands encircled hers and instantly fused her with warmth. Her first instinct was to pull away. Just the feel of his fingers intertwined with hers dug up so many memories. The first time they met, went to dinner, a movie. The first time he'd held her hand during a stroll in the park after ice cream. She'd known then she was falling hard for Bridge Spencer and hadn't cared about how they'd build a relationship with him frequently being undercover with the FBI and her CIA job often sending her into foreign countries. None of that mattered.

All she'd wanted was to spend her life with Bridge Spencer on his ranch in Texas. She'd had every intention of walking away from the Agency. Until Charlie Wingbender had been murdered and she'd been framed with a deep-fake video—her body and face replacing the true killer's.

"I'm not tired either. Just cold," he whispered. "We need to exit this mountain as soon as daylight comes. I know my team is searching for us. I check in every evening around six. Didn't last night, and by now the camp has notified Molly's uncle about her disappearance, and that I'm missing too. I suspect they're out here searching for us as well. I imagine some people from the camp might be out here too, or will be once it's daylight."

"I need to send word to David that Molly's safe. I don't want him to catch wind I'm out here and think I've come to hurt either of you."

His grin sent a swirl into her belly. "You kind of did. I have two lacerations and some bruises to prove it."

She snickered. "I warned you."

"I'm not a great listener. David mentioned to

us that people had been after the Mask program and that Molly's previous attempted abduction might have something to do with that. The details of the program were above his knowledge, so it's above ours too. But he seems to be right, and you will be the number one suspect."

She feared exactly that. As far as listening, Bridge was hardheaded no doubt but he had been one of the best listeners, always lending an ear to her. It was one of the things she'd loved best about him. He was confident but not cocky, knowledgeable but not a know-it-all. And he'd been a complete gentleman, which was why she knew he'd never really hurt her, even when he'd clocked her jaw. "I'm worried a phantom has been planted in the Wingbender household. Might have been there since before me. Anderson was always a few steps ahead. I've been racking my brain trying to figure out who it was but that's the thing about phantoms."

"You never know when you're in the presence of one."

"Exactly. Molly had tutors and then there were the employees of the Wingbender estate. From the grounds to inside the house that's at least forty people or more. But it's the only way to know Molly was here. If David sent her here to be safe and hired you, then he wouldn't have told anyone where she was, except someone he trusted. Is there any way one of your—"

"No. No moles in Spears & Bow." He was adamant. "You met Axel Spears a few times. He's a stand-up guy with more integrity than anybody I know and whoever he trusts, I do too."

She believed him. Bridge would have vetted everyone on his new team and he had excellent discernment. It was a gift. "Who all is on the team? I'm simply curious now, making conversation."

"How did you hear she was here?" He ignored her question.

"Talia got wind and before you say it, I trust her completely."

Bridge arched his eyebrows but said nothing.

"Now about that new job," she said, leading him back to the subject she'd introduced.

"Axel Spears and his colleague cofounded the company and brought in former Secret Service Agent Libby Winters. She's tough as nails and fearless, though she's seen near-death multiple times. Amber Rathbone is a former homicide detective with the Memphis PD. She has good instincts, and is a better shot than you."

"Trying to make me jealous?" Wendy teased. "That's a pretty perfect shot."

He released her now-warm hands and shifted

into a more comfortable position. "You'd like her. She's almost as snarky as you."

"I like her already. That all?"

"No," he said and scrunched his nose, then smoothed one of her hairs behind her ear. "It's tickling my nose."

His gesture tickled her heart.

"Axel's cofounder is someone you might know. Former CIA. I've never personally met him. Only Zoom calls. He works behind the scenes."

"Former CIA. Gadget guy or spy guy?"

"Spy. Archer Crow."

Wendy's heart skipped a beat and her mouth turned dry.

Did she know Archer Crow? Oh yeah she did.

He was the CIA's best and most skilled agent. And their top phantom.

"What is it?" Bridge asked. Wendy's face had shifted but she'd recovered quickly. Only someone who knew her well would have even caught the minuscule flash in her eyes and the twitch of her lips. Had she and Archer been a thing before? His blood turned green at that thought. She and Archer working together on a spy mission, so closely it developed into intimate feelings for one another and then a romantic relationship. Not that Bridge should care; he didn't. He and Wendy were never getting back together. She would rather be a lone wolf than call on him for help. She'd crushed him in ways he'd never recover from.

He'd never been more transparent with anyone in his life, and that included his siblings, and they were all tight. After three years his heart was as shredded as it was the day he read her letter. It had been a coward's way out when she was no coward. At least not physically.

She had definitely been a coward in matters of the heart.

"Nothing. Just nothing."

He let it go. But it was obvious she'd had some kind of relationship with Archer. Since he'd forced her to back off the probing into his resignation from the FBI, he wasn't going to be hypocritical and press her now. "Once we're off this mountain, we might be able to contact someone from my team to hack into the system on the dark web and shut down the ad." But the only one he knew who could do that was Archer Crow. He had to move past this jealous outburst. He was an almost forty-year-old man, not some high school jock ticked that his old girlfriend was dating the new quarterback. Her life before him or after him was her own.

Being this close was almost unbearable. All those memories flooded into his brain. Memories he'd pushed deep into a locked compartment he never allowed himself to open. All of them were unlodging now like a burst dam. Was it as challenging for her? She didn't appear to be struggling with their forced proximity. Or maybe she covered it up better than him.

"So you like working for them?" she asked, rerouting the Archer Crow conversation.

"Like I said, this is my first assignment. Axel was hounding me for a while, but I wasn't ready. Stone, as you know, had started an aftermath recovery business and I decided to help him. Rhode joined and Sissy, but she mostly does the grief counseling. She remarried not long ago. Beau Brighton if you can believe that."

"Really? Good for her. Texas royalty."

"Stone married too."

She covered her laugh with her hands. "Who is putting up with his mean muggin' face?"

"Another Texas Ranger. Emily O'Connell. She's as hardheaded if not more than him. It's fun watching them. Rhode has twins and recently married."

Her eyebrows rose, and Bridge shared how his brother, in his dark despair, had made a mistake and had a one-night stand that ended in twins. But he and Teegan were together now and married. Happy. Things had fallen into place for all his siblings. Even his mom was in remission. Not quite considered cancer-free yet, but doing very well. He missed Dad and Paisley though; the years never grew easier after losing a loved one. Which was why he'd finally accepted the job with Spears & Bow. He needed something too. To move forward physically even if his heart had paused and not caught up.

He'd been stuck so long.

"Wow. I never expected Rhode to settle down. I'm glad he finally did."

At her words a wall of tense silence built between them. They were supposed to have settled down and raised a family together. Was she thinking about that too? Did it crush and devastate her as it did him or did she not give it a thought?

"Yeah." Her signature soft scent wafted into his nostrils and tightened his belly. Lying this close to her was too hard. Too much. He swallowed hard. "How do you think Molly is doing?" He needed a distraction from being inches away from her, smelling her.

"It's hard to say but what should frighten her doesn't necessarily. She's logical, which works in our favor. But I'm terrified for her. What if a bullet intended for me hits her? Or she runs off and gets lost out here? I can't… I wouldn't be able to forgive myself."

Bridge knew all about those feelings. He'd lost eight-year-old Levi James. He'd never forget that mission in Atlanta, going undercover in a child-trafficking ring. Everything went sideways fast and Levi had died by a bullet intended for Bridge. Then on the way out with the lifeless boy, an agent he'd recruited and trained died in an explosion. After all that work to find and rescue Levi, he'd died anyway, and Bridge had nightmares every night about that sweet boy. He'd been mad at himself, then mad at God, then back to just being mad at himself.

He'd wanted to bring Levi home alive. And he'd failed him.

He couldn't fail Molly.

"We'll do our very best, Wendy. I like her. She's quirky and cool."

Wendy smiled and Bridge saw in her eyes the warmth and affection she felt for the child. It was one of the many things he'd adored about Wendy—her compassion and love for children. Her tough and demanding job hadn't jaded her. And even now, when she appeared more cynical, the care for Molly was still burning bright. At least that trait hadn't been tainted.

"She is. I enjoyed being her nanny. I've been trying to think of the people I came in contact with who could have been a phantom working for Anderson, but they were either that good or there isn't one."

Bridge didn't want to mention Talia, the tech

analyst, still worked on the inside. CIA double agents weren't just a thing of books and movies. She could be the leak. He'd tuck it away for now though. It was possible Talia wasn't sharing information intentionally but trusted someone else who might be doublecrossing her and their country.

Instead he said, "We need to stop giving any information to anyone until you and I can figure things out. Except for my team. I have to check in with them."

Wendy frowned. "That's not fair. I have to trust who you trust but you can't trust the people or rather the one person I do? Do you think Talia is backstabbing me?"

So much for keeping this to himself. "I didn't say that."

"You didn't have to." She huffed. "And here I thought we might be able to put our past behind us and work together in a friendly fashion. I see that's not the case."

His ire rose. She could compartmentalize their relationship—turn it off like a water faucet and pretend it never happened. It clearly hadn't meant as much to her as it had to him. "I can be civil, Wendy. But we are not friends and we will never be friends. We can work together but I'm not going to follow your orders like a puppy in training. And I am over being in this confining space with you." He reached over her to unzip the bag, and instantly regretted it as his nose connected with hers and his lips grazed over her mouth, stirring up all new feelings he wished he hadn't.

She jerked back. "I got it. Just be patient. You never were patient," she griped.

"You want to keep score?" he hissed. She was driving him mad as they fought to unzip the bag, neither of them succeeding, their limbs tangling with one another. "Be still! You're going to wake Molly."

"Don't tell me what to do," she whispered back and he felt the fire behind the words.

"Or what?" he dared her.

Her elbow jabbed his ribs. "You don't want to start something you can't finish, Bridge Alejandro Spencer."

Oh she did not middle name him. "That's it. I've had it." He flipped on top of her and pinned her arms over her head with one hand while fumbling for the sleeping bag zipper with the other.

She laughed but there was zero humor involved. "You think pinning my wrists is going to be enough to hold me?"

No. It would take titanium force to keep her down. But he was going to be the one to unzip this stupid sleeping bag. There was more at stake here than freedom from covers.

"Nope." And without thinking it through he claimed her lips, throwing her off guard and stilling her into a paralyzed state. She wasn't expecting that and he would never in any other kind of circumstance kiss a woman without permission but he needed this little victory of unzipping the bag and walking away and this was the only way he knew to do it. She'd done all the walking away before. She'd rendered him useless and he needed some power back. He needed to be able to walk away this time.

He regretted his action immediately. This wasn't gentlemanly behavior at all and his mama had raised him better. But then she surprised him. Her body relaxed and she kissed him back. Stunning him. Now he was paralyzed. He hadn't expected that. He'd expected her to kick his butt but he'd hoped to get the zipper free first.

Her kiss was familiar but fresh. Like cool water to his parched lips. Like the first decadent bite of a chocolate cake you'd been eyeing and salivating over all day.

Then he heard the zipper slide.

Zzztt...

And Wendy broke the kiss. "There. You can go now."

His breath was ragged and his brain full of

fuzz. For a moment he thought they'd shared something real, something solid. Even if it had started under false pretenses. But she was simply playing him at his own game. When had his hands tangled in her hair? He removed them, raised himself up off her and headed for the makeshift shelter door.

He'd made a huge mistake but then she'd taken it to a new level. She'd grabbed a toehold of his heart only to crush it in her palm. And he had no one to blame but himself.

He'd started it.

"Wait, Bridge," she said. "I'm—"

But she never got to finish her remark. Gunfire cracked through the night and right through the shelter door branches.

SIX

Wendy sprang to her feet, diving over Molly. "Come on, Molly. Wake up. We have to go. Now." There was no time to grab the blankets. They had to move. Move. Move. She slung her backpack on and shoved Molly's on her as she shielded her. "Bridge, talk to me," she hollered and clung to her Glock.

"Sniper."

Another shot came too close for comfort and she brought Molly out of the shelter, continuing to stay in front of her. "Night goggles?"

"Don't know. Don't want to get close enough to find out. Let's move. East. Run." They darted through the trees, Bridge leading the charge and Wendy keeping Molly covered. She prayed God would shield the sweet girl and keep her safe as they dodged through the trees. The sniper had flushed them out. How many were in waiting? Where were they? Her heart jackhammered as she kept to the trees for coverage.

The ground was covered in several inches of snow and it was still falling fast. The only upside was it might cover up their tracks before the sniper could find them.

"Are we going to die?" Molly asked matter-of-factly.

"No." She wasn't sure to be honest but no sounded like the better answer because if she had anything to do with it, no one was dying but the bad guys. "Your dad's program is very important and a lot of bad people want it. I know it's inside your head and will keep you safe. But you can't ever tell anyone unless I tell you that you can, okay?" Molly was a rule follower and never broke one. She needed the caveat that she could tell if Wendy said she could.

"Okay. Daddy said I had to keep it a secret until it was time to reveal it. Daddy is dead. Is it time?"

"When I say it's time. For now, we are going to keep you and all that's in your big brain a secret."

"Brains aren't big. The human adult brain weighs about three pounds. That's less than an average newborn baby. Not counting premature babies."

"Right. Of course," Wendy said, thankful that Molly was distracted with other facts and not the most important one—that someone was shooting at them. "Bridge, if I'm supposed to be taken in alive, why are we being shot at?"

"Because you were right the first time. They're flushing us out and maybe leading us somewhere. Or maybe they're trying to take me out in order to get to you." His voice was calm but he was a pro and any fear he might be feeling would be masked. "Let's go."

They raced farther through the dense foliage, their feet crunching on the powdery snow. The incline was steadily creeping upward. This was not going down the mountain. No other choice at the moment though. They had to keep moving.

"Hey, I think that's a cave ahead. Stay here and I'll go check it out." Bridge tossed Wendy a glance and she gave him a thumbs-up. He disappeared into the darkness as she and Molly crouched low in a thicket of branches. Soon he low-whistled and she took Molly's backpack.

"Come on."

She followed the whistle and made it to a crag in the mountain. "Is that a cave or a crevice?" she asked him as she surveyed the narrow opening.

"Cave, but it's a tight squeeze for a few feet before it opens up. Can you manage it?"

She nodded but trepidation sent her heart racing and her cheeks heated. Wendy may not like it, but she would do it. He motioned for her and

Molly to hurry inside. Wendy slipped in first, then helped Molly inside and Bridge followed behind. "I found a branch and propped it up at the entrance as camouflage. Let's hope it works because while I hope there's another way out, I don't know that for sure."

While it was freezing in the cave, and damp, it was still warmer than outside and without the thermal blankets, they were in big trouble. Maybe they could double back at dawn's first light and secure them. But anyone could be waiting them out to return, especially once they saw equipment had been left. Important camping equipment.

Bridge shined his small flashlight around the cave. Running water had frozen to the cave walls, glistening like glass, and water puddles and bat guano dotted the uneven rocky floor.

"It's cold in here," Molly stated. "You can start fires in caves but it can also be dangerous because of methane levels."

"True," Wendy said. "But we'll take our chances because we have to stay warm. Do we know when the snow is going to stop?"

"No." Bridge massaged the back of his neck. "Instead of heading down the mountain, we've gone up, which means it'll take us more time having to backtrack."

"Well, thanks, Captain Obvious."

"Bridge isn't a captain. Are you a captain, Bridge?" Molly asked.

"No. She's saying I'm stating information we already know."

Molly ran a gloved hand across her runny nose. "Oh. Well, that's true. You did do that."

Wendy chuckled and Bridge snorted but the smirk was there. On those full lips with a perfect cupid's bow. Lips that had kissed her earlier. She had been startled by it and she'd like to say it came unwelcomed but only one of those would be true. While it had been unexpected, her response had been even more unexpected. The instant his lips touched hers, old familiar feelings she'd hadn't allowed herself to think on in years resurfaced. The way he was tender and kind. Giving and not taking. Patient and not greedy. That's what responded. Her heart's memory. The way even in just a kiss, she felt safe and cherished. Every embrace, linked fingers and kiss came from a display of care, consideration, respect and love.

This time he'd had a motive. He wanted to unzip the bag and run away. Wendy suspected something else was going on but the kiss reminded her how empty she'd been without him and how much she'd missed him, and it terrified her.

She couldn't let her emotions compromise this

mission. Right now, her life was burned. Erased. She was a fugitive. Wendy had no life to offer Bridge. Even if she dreamed of how returning to his arms would be, how she'd beg for his forgiveness for destroying him. In her imagined scenarios he always forgave her and welcomed her back.

But it was clear Bridge wasn't interested in them picking up where they left off, except that kiss... She'd felt the emotion on his lips. Or maybe she simply wanted to. She was reading more into it than it was—what she might have wished for once upon a time.

Too much time had passed. Absence hadn't made his heart grow fonder, but had hardened it, so much that he'd claimed they weren't even friends. Forced civility remained in the wake of what she'd done, and it hurt but she owned it. His feelings were valid and she deserved to be shut out. The pain she'd indirectly inflicted, after promising she would never hurt him, had left an open wound in her soul as much as it had left one in his.

Bridge had dated a woman before her, and it had grown serious. He had been contemplating a proposal when he'd caught her cheating with one of her task force members in the Bureau. He had been shredded, his heart a bloody mess. His only saving grace had been Rena hadn't worked for CIRG, and he didn't have to see her often.

For Wendy, gaining Bridge's trust had taken months and even then he'd been wary since her job was built on deception and manipulation—not exactly points in her favor but it was the job and those tactics saved lives and the country. Bridge knew that deep down Wendy was not those things and she'd finally earned his trust and his heart. After, they fell fast and hard and forever.

Or so she thought.

She admitted to handling things horribly, but she'd wanted to protect Bridge—and his family—and she had done it the only way she knew how. Anderson had power and deep pockets. He wasn't a man to be underestimated and he would not hesitate to harm Bridge or his family members in order to force Wendy's hand. She'd loved him and the Spencers too much to let anything happen to them, and she'd taken the easy way out with a letter. Looking into Bridge's face would have been too agonizing and she might have caved and let him run with her or try to help. But he couldn't help her.

She had been acutely aware that after reading the letter, he would never trust or love her again, and might not love or trust any woman again but she'd prayed that wasn't the case. She wanted him to be happy and if it meant with another woman who wouldn't bring trouble to him and the family, then so be it. Now, it was too late to fix. They couldn't go back, couldn't change the past, and they had no way forward either—not with each other.

As regret and sadness threatened to swamp her, she was saved by Molly's voice echoing in the cave.

"I need to use the bathroom, Nanny Wendy."

She fumbled through her backpack for toiletries. "Let's move farther into the cave and find a spot for privacy while Bridge is collecting firewood." Wendy led Molly deeper into the cave, using her little lantern from her backpack. "Molly, are you scared?"

"Yes."

"I'm going to keep you and Mr. Bridge safe. Are you feeling antsy?" She quickly corrected her wording. "I mean, are you overstimulated since you're out of your routine and schedule?"

"Yes." Her sweet little face showed no emotion but inside Wendy knew she was like a pent-up puppy with no way to channel the anxious energy.

"I brought you something that might help calm your anxiety and overstimulation." She reached into the backpack and brought out a fidget spinner. She handed it to her in her favorite color—yellow.

"Thank you, Nanny Wendy. I also need toilet paper."

Wendy smiled. "Right. Yes." She handed her a roll and let her take the lantern into an off-shoot of the cave. "I'll be right out here waiting for you."

Molly headed into the cave's recesses and with it, the light. Wendy had never been a big fan of caves. As a child she'd hated the dark, but in her training as a CIA officer she'd overcome that childhood fear. Darkness was void, colorless. Like her world without Bridge. But she had the Lord and He had been a source of great comfort when she'd been in North Korea especially. He filled her heart to overflowing, but He'd also created her to want earthly relationships and she'd wanted that with Bridge. Seeing him unearthed the ache she'd tried to bury—no, erase.

But a man like him had a way of writing himself in permanent ink on a person's heart.

She hoped he was safe out there collecting wood. How long would they be safe in here? If they were breached from the crag that opened into the cave, and there was no other way out, then it wouldn't end well. There had to be another way out. If Molly wasn't with her, she'd explore farther and look for a second exit. But caves often were dangerous and taking a child on that kind of expedition would be reckless.

After a few moments Molly returned requesting hand sanitizer and they traveled back to the mouth of the cave where she found a dry spot to sit and play with her fidget spinner. Bridge had already brought in some wood he'd found and must be out searching for more to keep them going through the rest of the night. Molly had to be exhausted. She wasn't used to this kind of fast pace. Wendy was used to little sleep and running on fumes. One had to be in her line of work.

"Molly, are you hungry?"

"Not particularly. My stomach isn't growling. That's how I usually know I'm hungry."

Oh, what would it be like to only eat when you were truly hungry? Wendy had a penchant for sugary treats when she was bored or down or happy. Okay, she was an emotional eater. She shouldn't be but on occasion she caught herself drowning in ice cream instead of God's word. The latter was better for her and fewer calories. For the most part she tried to eat healthy with the amount of workouts she needed to do in order to stay in top condition. She needed stamina and strength to be a spy but she had to admit having babies and getting soft in the middle was her dream. It meant less time fighting bad guys and more time fighting laundry, which was far less stressful than this.

Bridge entered the cave and dropped a stack

of limbs by the crag, then used the branches to cover the opening so anyone looking for them wouldn't notice. Or so they hoped.

"I should have enough to get us through the night and I brought in some pine branches to lay down to make it more comfortable than rock. It's no luxury hotel bed but it's better than nothing." He sighed and began piling small branches and logs to form a teepee. "Please tell me you have a lighter or matches or something. I really don't want to do this the hard way." His tone was polite but not friendly.

"I do." She dug into her backpack aka survival kit that she always carried and handed him a fire starter.

"Here's to us not blowing up from methane buildup."

She didn't smell methane but that didn't mean it wasn't permeating the cave. She prayed for a small mercy and the flames danced, but they remained unharmed. "Praise God," she whispered and arranged some softer pine branches for Molly to sit on near the fire. She shrugged out of her insulated coat and laid it down as a pillow. "Try to rest, Molly. We'll have to hike out at first light. That's a few hours away."

Molly obeyed quietly. She wasn't much of a conversationalist—a lot like her father, Charlie. Only when necessary and to correct someone.

The cold seeped into Wendy's bones without the protection of her waterproof coat and she sat on the other side of the fire, but she'd slept in far worse conditions than these.

The fire crackled and illuminated the cave, casting dancing shadows on the walls. The heat slowly warmed her chilled bones and she welcomed the feeling. But this was no campfire or outdoor vacation. Beyond this cave, multiple people hunted her. Molly would appear to be a casualty to them and Bridge an obstacle and a threat, which meant they'd take him out without hesitation. That scared her but she kept her fears locked up. For now this was about staying alive. Between the wild animals, elements and hired killers, their percentage of making it down the mountain was less than 50 percent. If she was alone, she might have a better chance.

She glanced at Molly, lying quietly with her eyes closed, only the fidget spinner making noise to prove she was awake. Bridge sat beside Molly, his bare hands stretched out over the fire as he scrutinized Wendy. She diverted her gaze to the crag that would free them from the cave.

"Don't even think about it, Wendy," he murmured and she returned her sight to his narrowed amber eyes and his square set jaw. He'd read her with complete ease. Bridge knew her better than anyone ever had—or would.

"I could find a cell signal and get help faster. These people don't want you or Molly. They want me."

"Nope."

"I could—"

"Nope."

This wasn't an argument or even a levelheaded conversation. Bridge wouldn't budge on this; she was going nowhere on his watch.

"And nope to attempting to secure me so you can escape. Let's not have another altercation. I won't be as kind as before."

Wendy rubbed her chin where he'd clipped her earlier and refrained from informing him that if she truly wanted to leave, he'd have no power to stop her. Bridge was physically stronger than her with over one hundred extra pounds of muscle on his frame, and it was muscle trained for combat. But she was smart, savvy and sprite. Brawn wasn't the only way to overpower an enemy. Sometimes one simply needed to outwit him.

"Maybe I won't be either," she returned, aware it would pull a rise out of him. She didn't enjoy irritating him, but it was easier to rumble than to reminisce. Good memories served to reveal all she'd lost, all they'd lost.

He poked at the fire, ignoring her barb, seemingly unwilling to stoop to her childish level, but instead he did something far worse. He ignored her, tending the wood and keeping a flame alight, leaving her to observe in silence and battle her unsettled feelings alone.

Molly's breathing evened out. Her thick dark hair spilled around her pink cheeks and her lips parted, relaxed and content. Molly was precious and dear to Wendy.

"You know anything about her mom?" Bridge whispered. "In her dossier, it mentioned she died when Molly was a baby."

"She did research and taught at Caltech. Charlie never spoke of her, and Molly has no memory of her. According to my intel, she disappeared when Molly was an infant."

"Died or vanished? Not the same thing."

"I don't know. All I do know is Molly has grown up with a string of nannies and a father who loved her but was so involved in his work, he neglected her. Neglected himself even. I can't count how many times Rita—his house manager—had to remind him to eat and that was with a sandwich in front of him. Crust turned hard before he took a bite. He was so absorbed in the Mask program."

"Was her specialty artificial intelligence too? That's a science, right?" Bridge asked and scooted farther back from the nice-sized fire. Smoke plumed and filtered out through the small opening in the cave, but her hair still reeked of wood smoke.

Wendy nodded. "I think so but she did other things too. She taught robotics. They have this prototype she designed that's kind of scary. It's so lifelike and it can calculate the needs of its primary person. You program it that way."

"I think I saw a horror movie like that. The doll was life-sized and took on a mind of its own. Not really but based on the programming. It was made to always see to the child's needs and protect her if it detected danger. The movie was horrifying, not because of the gore but the fact that this could happen. Our technology is so advanced and that's just what the public is privy to." Bridge shivered. "I don't know if we're better for it or not."

Wendy sighed. "I think, like anything, what is meant for good can always be used for evil. A lot of sinister things make its way across the web, like the ad taken out for me, but it also has provided a way to send the Gospel out to areas in a blink, so I'm glad we have it. Even if right now it's not working in my best interest."

"There's the positive person I once knew."

Knew. Not loved.

"I guess she still exists. But I've changed, Bridge." At his questioning look, she added, "And I really don't want to talk about it."

Bridge nodded once. "I understand. Just know that whatever happened to sour your outlook, it doesn't have to. But then I could take my own advice and I've rarely ever done that." He laughed. "Try to sleep if you can. I'm going to keep watch and the fire burning. The heavy snowfall will conceal those branches and us, as well as act as a barrier from the wind. Plus it'll mask the smoke some. We should be safe until first light."

"I'll try." She rested her head on the cave wall and closed her eyes. Hoping sleep would come and fearing it wouldn't.

Bridge studied Wendy as she dozed. He knew she'd never fall into a heavy sleep but she needed rest. They all did. Especially Molly. This couldn't be easy on her. Poor kid had lost so much in her short ten years. A mom. A dad. Now she was running for her life in the mountains and didn't understand what was happening. Neither did Bridge. Not really. He feared what might happen if Anderson retrieved all the pieces of the code. He would definitely have Wendy assassinated and probably steal Molly away for her knowledge, and a man as corrupt as he was would possibly use her for other projects. She'd become a guinea pig. An unsuspecting weapon because of her bright mind and photographic memory. He would never let that happen. Bridge would die before letting harm come to Molly or Wendy.

He stoked the fire, which was a nice size and warming up the mouth of the cave. Unfortunately they couldn't hole out here waiting for the cavalry to arrive. No one knew exactly where to find them. They needed to get off this mountain and get a cell signal.

But a hit had been put out and once they reached civilian life, they were no safer than on this mountain. Hunters could be everywhere. Over four million dollars was a big incentive. His thoughts drifted as his eyes grew heavy. It was almost 2:00 a.m.

A sound woke him from his light dozing. Not outside the cave, but from inside. Bridge blinked, hoping to see into the inky cave as stirring and clicking echoed along the cave flooring, like when Rhode's dogs' nails clicked along the hardwood flooring at the ranch.

Wendy bolted upright, gun in hand while Molly continued to snooze, lightly snoring. "What is that?" she whispered as she jumped to her feet and began securing their gear for a fast exit.

"I'm not sure but it doesn't sound human."

"Well, I don't like that."

Neither did Bridge. "Hey, Molly." He shook her, rousing her from sleep. She moaned and rolled over, flicking his hand away. While he understood the sweet pleasure of sleep, they might have to hightail it out of here. He nudged her again as the sound came closer.

That's when he heard the bellowing and chuffing.

SEVEN

Bridge helped a still-sleeping and stumbling Molly to her feet just as a massive black bear entered from the backside of the cave. "Slowly inch your way to the crag," he told Wendy as he handed off the child to her. He knew if this bear decided to take a run at them, they'd never all make it through. He'd do whatever he could to make sure Molly and Wendy got out.

"Hey, bear! Hey! Scat! Scat!" Bridge shouted and clapped his hands hoping to frighten the beast, but it wasn't at all terrified. This mountain led to a tourist town where bears were often fed and photographed. The fear of humans was gone due to their coexisting.

The bear clawed and chuffed again, threatening them. Wendy slowly backed away with Molly beside her.

"Help her out first, then you go. I'm right behind."

Wendy's eyes didn't seem to show she believed him.

The bear rose on its back paws and let out a deafening roar, echoing against the walls and sending a shiver through Bridge. "Do you have bear spray?"

"Yes, but I can't get into my backpack right now. Let me help Molly out first."

They didn't have that kind of time. The bear was only about thirty feet away from them and pretty ticked. Bridge kept his eyes on the bear, showing no fear and standing taller. "Scat!" he shouted again, but the bear only rolled its head and snorted, pawing at the ground.

The sound of branches breaking let him know Molly was out of the cave. A zipper being undone rattled the bear and it rose up again. This time it was done threatening them.

It charged Bridge and he turned to run, bumping straight into Wendy. The can of bear spray fell to the cave floor and began rolling away.

"Get out of here," he hollered but Wendy dove for the spray can instead as the bear barreled toward them, close enough Bridge smelled the musky scent and saw long white teeth flashing in the dimly lit cave.

Suddenly it roared and pawed at its face. "Go!" Wendy bellowed and Bridge hightailed it through the crag, yanking Wendy with him. The frigid air stole his breath. And all that warmth from the fire was gone in an instant. Molly stood with her hands in her coat pockets and her stocking cap pulled down low. Wendy was bent over, breathing hard.

A paw with sharp claws pushed through the crevice and Wendy shrieked and jumped back, clutching her chest. "Wasn't expecting that. Can it squeeze through there?"

"I don't want to stick around and find out." Bridge took Molly's hand. "You okay, champ?"

"I didn't win anything. Champ is short for champion. I prefer proper language."

Bridge stifled a reaction. He'd been afraid the child was traumatized but she was still the same Molly. "Glad you're okay." He reached out to touch her but remembered she wasn't a fan of physical affection. "Let's be going." Just because they'd escaped a bear, it didn't mean they were safe. Other predators were out there. The human kind. "Down the mountain. We might find more cabins closer to the towns below."

Wendy nodded. "Agreed."

"Are your feet warm, Molly?" Bridge asked. She'd had on riding boots, which were sturdy and tall but not insulated. The weather was below freezing and the snow was now up to her mid-calves and his ankles. This trek was dangerous for all of them but especially a child. He prayed God would keep them all safe.

Molly nodded.

Good. For now she was okay but he wasn't sure how far they'd have to hike and in this weather time wasn't working on their side. He took the lead while Wendy brought up the rear, but he didn't like not having eyes on her. She was capable and strong but he felt responsible for all their safety. Their feet crunched snow and climbed over fallen trees and bramble as they marched on. The only thing that might be in their favor was the fact an intelligent person would seek shelter in this weather, which meant the host of assassins after them would be hunkered down until first light too.

Or at least he hoped they would.

They marched for about thirty minutes down the mountain until a looming shadow came into view in the distance. "Praise God. A cabin." Bridge could have dropped to his knees in tears of joy and relief. His own feet were starting to go numb and his face was on fire, likely in early stages of frostbite. "I'll go check it out, and you two hang back. Don't want to surprise anyone who might be inside, whether owners, renters or the people after us."

"Or I can go and you can stay behind," Wendy offered.

He ignored her proposition. "Give me ten minutes. If I don't whistle, run."

Wendy frowned. "If you don't whistle, I'm coming in for you. End of story. Go. Clock's ticking."

Bridge growled under his breath but took off in a jog, keeping to the shadows as he approached the dark cabin. It was small, but not what he'd consider a shanty. No cars. But a road must cut up through here somewhere, now covered by snow. Or a person could have brought a side-by-side up here through off-roading. That was more likely. He peeped in one of the side windows but it was too dark to see inside. He made one sweep around the cabin, then slowly climbed the sagging porch, listening for any movement inside.

Dead silence.

His heart beat hard against his ribs and he retrieved his gun, then opened the screen door with a screechy yawn. Flinching, he waited a beat. No new sounds or movement. He turned the handle and to his surprise it was unlocked. Opening the door with quiet and slow precision, he entered the cold cabin. The scent of musk and earth whacked his senses. No one had been here in a while but that wasn't a bad thing. He used his tiny flashlight and scanned the area. It was an open floor plan with a cozy living room and small kitchen. Looked like one bedroom and no bathroom. He wasn't surprised to see no plumbing in this rugged terrain. Definitely a hunting cabin.

Walking back to the porch he cupped his hands around his mouth and gave a low whistle. In a few moments Wendy and Molly hustled up the porch and into the cabin.

"It smells bad in here," Molly said. "I don't like it."

"Neither do I," Wendy said. "I think an animal died in here and no one has been inside to air it out in a long time." She dug into her backpack again and brought out an army green scarf. "Here. Tie this around your face to help mask the scent until your nose gets used to it."

Molly wrapped the scarf around her face till nothing remained but her big doe eyes.

"Better?"

"Yes," Molly said through the material. "And my nose isn't cold anymore."

"Good." Wendy smiled and then surveyed their surroundings. "Wood-burning stove. Stack of wood. You want to handle that or me?" she asked Bridge.

"I got it."

"I'll see if there are any supplies we can take with us at dawn." She turned to Molly. "Why don't you lie down on the couch? It'll probably smell but it's better than a cave floor."

"Okay." Molly did as she was instructed and curled into a ball on the old brown couch.

"Close the curtains, Wendy, and I'll switch on that battery-operated lantern. Maybe they have extra batteries."

Wendy closed the few curtains that weren't already drawn, and Bridge switched on a lantern. He went to work loading wood into the wood-burning stove and lit it. "Should warm us up in no time."

A cabinet door opened and he turned to see Wendy rummaging through them. "There's canned food and other supplies like a first-aid kit, toilet paper, thermoses." She opened another cabinet. "A few packs of individual snack crackers and cereal cups and they're not expired. Excellent." She tossed Bridge a pack of peanut butter crackers and asked Molly what she would like.

"I will take Goldfish crackers."

Wendy handed her a pack and then went back to the kitchen. "Yes! A case of bottled water." She brought them each a water, then sat on the couch. Bridge sat on the floor by the fire and they ate their snacks like it was a feast and downed a bottle of water each.

"I can warm water on the stove here and we

can put it in the thermos when we head out so we have something warm to drink," Bridge said as he finished off his peanut butter crackers. He was still ravenous but they needed to ration the food. No telling how long they might be stuck up here. Hopefully not long; it just depended on the obstacles coming at them in the morning.

"I'm going to check the bedroom and see if we can use any blankets or towels." Wendy walked into the bedroom and Bridge sighed. "You want anything else to eat?" he asked Molly.

"No thank you."

"You want to sleep in the bed?"

"No, the couch is fine. I don't like people sleeping by me. I need space." She took out her fidget spinner that Wendy had given her and he let her be. It was pretty clear she was needing quiet and Bridge worried all this trauma might send her into a meltdown or an inner shutdown. Neither of which was good or healthy.

"I'm going to check on Nanny Wendy. You be okay here?"

"Yes." She continued staring at the spinner while she worked it to make noise and spin.

Bridge entered the bedroom. In it were a queen-sized bed, a chest of drawers and one night table with a big lantern on it.

"I found batteries in the night table drawer so that's awesome." She turned on the lantern and the room lit up. It was clean and on the bed was a heavy green quilt with bears embroidered around the edges. "I also found a sleeping bag in the closet. We can take it for Molly. The quilt is too big to fold down into a backpack. But she'll be warm and that's all I care about. It's thermal too."

"Good. God does provide, doesn't He?"

She smiled. "He does. Since I dozed in the cave, I'll take first watch and you can have the bed. Get some shut-eye. It might be the last chance we get."

He wasn't going to argue; he was exhausted. But before he fell asleep, there was something he needed to do. Address their kiss in the makeshift shelter. "I need to apologize for earlier. I've done two things that were wrong so far and I'm sorry. One, I punched you in the face and then I kissed you without permission. You know I'm not some cave man or a bully. I won't let that happen again."

Wendy's face flushed and she glanced at the floor as if it were mesmerizing. "I know you're not that kind of man, Bridge. And I did kiss you back."

"To unzip the bag first."

"So that unsolicited kiss wasn't a ploy for you to unzip it first? You meant it…had feeling behind it?" She finally looked into his eyes and held them captive, searching.

What should he tell her? He decided to go with the truth because he was a grown man, and games were childish and petty. "I'm not okay, Wendy. I haven't been okay since you walked out and decided not to trust me or to at least give me the chance to help you or decide not to. You just walked out with my heart and all the power. And it's like seeing me again means absolutely nothing to you. So I wanted to be the one to unzip that sleeping bag and walk out on my own. First. I wanted some power back but you always have to put up a fight or be right, and the only way I knew to stun you was to do the one thing you'd never expect me to do. The one thing you wouldn't see coming. I acted on impulse."

Wendy didn't move. Didn't speak. Her face was unreadable, and he hated it.

"I didn't expect for it to hit me here." He made a fist and tapped his chest. "I forgot what I was actually trying to do and then you went and did it for me. I know it didn't mean anything to you. That's fine."

She opened her mouth to speak but Bridge held out his hand to halt her.

"No, really it's fine. There's no reason to try and smooth the awkwardness between us. Let it be. Let it go. I'm going to help you off this mountain and see that Molly is safe and then go on with my life."

Her lips tightened and her jaw worked but she nodded once. "That's all I ever wanted after I left. For you to move on and be happy again. Are you? Happy?"

That was the million-dollar question. God had been so faithful and good to him through all the pain and grief he'd felt after Wendy left him. What hurt the most was the feeling of betrayal. She betrayed their love by not trusting him to let her go or help her. A letter? She could have called even. But no. "I have happy days. Happy moments. But I loved you—and you know how hard it was for me to trust you, then to let myself fall in love with you. I have never loved anyone more in my life, including Rena. I don't know that I'm happy but I'm at peace. Now that I know you're safe, I might be able to find happiness again." Maybe. He was done with dating. He'd lost too much. Hurt too deep. He wasn't sure it was worth it.

"Then after this is settled and Molly is safe, I'll be in the wind and you'll know I'm alive and well and you can find it again. I'm sure someone is out there who won't trample over your heart. I'm sorry that I did. I never meant to." Her bottom lip quivered and she sucked it into her mouth. "I'll go keep watch. Get some sleep."

And she walked away. No feelings exposed. She was sorry she'd trampled his heart. But no mention she was sorry she left.

Wendy patrolled the small cabin, peeping out into the night as the wind howled and moaned creating an eerie horror movie vibe that they were living at the moment. Everyone knew in most horror movies, the heroine didn't find her happily-ever-after because the love interest always died. Bridge wasn't dead, but he'd made it clear a future together was. She didn't deserve a second chance if he'd give her one anyway. She stood by her decision to protect them by leaving them and going at this alone, but it was the way in which she left that she regretted. Bridge had deserved an in-person conversation. An explanation. In the end his family and Bridge were safe and she couldn't ask for more.

And now he had the closure he always wanted and could forge ahead in his life.

What about her? Could she move on? If her name was cleared and she could reenter society, what would she do with her life? Wendy was sure she was done with the CIA but she didn't actually know how to do anything else and she had no friends, no family.

She'd only had Bridge and the Spencers.

God would provide. She had no idea how or

when but she'd learned that often He bypassed her expectations with something she hadn't anticipated. And even in these crazy hard times He'd been her only constant. He wasn't going to abandon her now. Even if it felt at times He was so far off and impersonal.

She noticed Molly shivering and lightly knocked on Bridge's bedroom door to retrieve a blanket. He didn't answer so she slipped inside. He was under the covers fast asleep. He'd always looked like a little boy when he was sleeping and she remembered often watching him nap on the couch and dreaming of what their own little boy might look like if they were granted one. She'd hoped he would be just like Bridge. She slipped a blanket from the closet and paused.

Was that a shadow or something else outside the window? Her blood turned cold and she kept her feet planted to the old wood flooring, watching, straining to see through the heavy snow falling in white pillowy sheets. Maybe her paranoid mind was playing tricks on her.

She eased into the living room and placed the blanket over Molly, then she added a log to the fire in the wood-burning stove. Pulling on her coat, gloves and hat, she retrieved her gun and bear spray, then carefully exited through the front door. The wind was bitter and sharp against her cheeks and nose, but she'd been to Siberia before so this was nothing in comparison.

First she surveyed the white terrain, noticing a few animal footprints—some bigger than others. Nothing she noted as human. The night was silent minus the wind shaking branches and howling. She edged off the porch and moved around to the side of the house with the bedroom. Keeping close to the cabin as a shield, she scanned the area where she thought she'd seen the shadow of a person. Nothing moved or stirred. Nothing but stretching shadows of tree limbs.

No footprints.

Wendy then crept under the windows and along the cabin, moving around the back and crouching, watching. Observing. She might not see a person but she felt eyes watching her and a chill ran down her spine. If she were on the prowl for a target and found a cabin, she'd keep an eye on it too.

Staying on high alert, she then completed circling the cabin and froze. She was right.

Tracks, human tracks, had been made in the snow. But where was the watcher now? Should she wake Bridge and make a run for it? No. They had to stay and fight. Molly needed sleep and warmth. She and Bridge would have to stand their ground. As she turned, a slice cut through the air. She ducked, but it was too late. An arrow penetrated her bulky coat, missing her flesh and pinning her to the wooden cabin.

From the shadows a sprite figure emerged with the bow and arrow drawn again. Wendy tugged on the arrow but it was embedded in the wood. She had only one choice. Quickly, she unzipped her coat and shrugged out of it as another arrow soared, clipping her left shoulder with a burning pain.

Thwpt! Another arrow let loose, barely missing her leg.

With no other choice, Wendy raised her gun and fired once.

That was all she needed. She was a better shot with a gun than the shooter with the arrows. She raced toward the figure and lifted the ski mask.

A woman.

She'd rendered her useless. She'd had no other choice. Wendy respected human life, all human life, and leaving her out here in the middle of nowhere for animals turned her stomach. Didn't matter this person was after her for money. Wendy never wanted to become a monster like the ones she dealt with every day in her line of work.

She dragged the body behind the cabin, pilfered through her pockets, taking money, bear spray, a thin rope and two granola bars, then laid her to rest in the snow, covering her to try and preserve her from animals. At the sound of feet crunching on snow, she spun and raised her gun.

"It's me!" Bridge. "I heard a gunshot." He raced to her and looked down at the woman. "You know her?"

"No."

"Any ID?"

"No."

"Where's your coat?"

"Pinned to the side of the cabin with an arrow." Wendy shivered and finished burying the body in the snowdrift, then she and Bridge jogged to the side of the cabin. He was able to pull the coat from the wood.

"You got any duct tape?" he asked her as he surveyed the tear.

"Yeah."

"You okay?" he asked and she finally looked up at him, registering his concern. "You're bleeding."

"Nothing to worry about. Come on. Let's hurry inside. Light will be here in about two hours. Did the gunshot wake Molly?"

"No. Just me. Scared me half to death when I called your name and didn't hear you. My heart's still racing."

At least he was concerned. Inside she found the duct tape and patched up her coat, then added another log to the fire. Poor Molly was out cold. Exhaustion and stress could do that to a person.

She took a bottle of water and drank greedily. "Where's that first-aid kit?"

"I put it in my backpack." His brows scrunched together. "It's in the bedroom. Come on."

Wendy followed him and he retrieved the first-aid kit. "You need a stitch?"

"I don't think so."

"You want me to look at it?"

No. But where it was she couldn't see well. "Yeah. If you don't mind."

"Not at all. You've got blood seeping through. Take off your shirt." He dug into the first-aid kit while she shrugged out of her shirt and rolled up her T-shirt sleeve so the upper shoulder was exposed. He turned and winced. "Not great. The arrow took a chunk but it's not deep." He paused before applying the antiseptic. "This will sting."

She'd been tortured in North Korea after being chased through Tokyo by one of their operatives and caught, so she could handle this. Gritting her teeth, she remained still and quiet while he cleaned and dressed the wound. "Okay," he said. "Right as rain."

Wendy peered up into his eyes as she rolled her T-shirt sleeve down. "Thank you. I appreciate your concern."

He held her gaze for several beats, then nodded as he let out a shaky breath and put some distance between them. She was a total train wreck inside.

"Why don't you take the bed and I'll keep watch now?" Bridge offered. "You've been through it."

Wendy wasn't going to argue. "Thanks." She slid into the side Bridge had been sleeping, catching his scent on the pillow and sheets. The smell was comforting and she settled in and closed her eyes. When the door clicked closed, she covered her head with the sheets and quilt and quietly let herself cry.

Assassins and bloody fights she could handle and hold her own against. Knowing the man she'd once so completely loved was in the room next to her and no longer belonged to her was as searing as being repeatedly ran through with a sword. More excruciating than a piercing arrow, a bullet burning through the flesh, waterboarding or even fire. It was a cold yet burning pain that suffocated her.

One she didn't know how to free herself from.

But she would. She had no choice.

She inhaled deeply, trying not to concentrate on Bridge's scent but regaining some composure and trying to sleep. She wasn't sure how long she had before another hired gun came calling.

Wendy had a lot of doubts, but none of them

was about being attacked again. That she knew was going to happen.

When she awoke, it was to the smell of smoke. She jolted out of the bed.

The cabin had been set on fire.

EIGHT

Wendy ran into the living room where Bridge was asleep, his head leaned back on the sofa cushion. Molly was still out, lightly snoring. "Bridge!" Wendy called and his eyes snapped open, red lines webbing in the whites of his eyes.

He breathed in and instantly jumped up. "We're being smoked out."

Smoked out so someone could play Capture the Flag with Wendy. She would not go down without a fight. "Molly, wake up. Come on, hon, you need to wake up." The first pops of light were coming over the horizon, not even a little color yet. Wendy shoved herself into her coat and tossed the backpack over her good shoulder.

"I'll go out first. Decoy. They won't shoot if they're trying to capture you."

Wendy did not like this idea even a little. "No, but they might realize you're not me and kill you to remove you and extract me. I have to go out first."

"We don't know what kind of trap lays ahead but it can't be close to the cabin. I did three perimeter sweeps, the last one only a few minutes ago."

"A lot can happen in a few minutes if you know what you're doing, Bridge."

He didn't argue with that.

"Why don't we go under?" Molly asked, rubbing her tired eyes with her gloved hands.

"Under how?" Wendy asked.

"Under the couch. It's cold." She pointed to the couch.

Bridge cocked his head. "She's right. I did feel cold air when I sat on the floor but I thought it was a draft coming in from under the front door."

"There's a handle under there," Molly said. "I felt it. When you and Bridge were in the bedroom."

Shoving the couch out of the way, Bridge grinned. "She's right." A floor panel had been cut out and a trap door put in its place.

"Of course I'm right. I don't lie or give information without facts. You need facts to support a claim or theory." Molly was standing with that confident gaze and using that matter-of-fact tone again. Wendy could hug her.

"How do we know it'll lead anywhere? If the house burns to the ground, we could be trapped," Wendy said.

The heat inside the house intensified as smoke poured in through the cracks and crevices. Wendy rushed to a window. Flames licked the side of the cabin. It was only a matter of seconds before it would eat up the wood and break through. In the kitchen pieces of shingles and roof fell to the floor. They didn't have time for someone to check the potential escape route. They had no other choice.

This would either work in their favor or seal their death warrants. Wendy's stomach knotted. She was willing to risk it all; she had nothing to lose. Molly and Bridge on the other hand had lives to live and people to go home to. People who loved them and would be devastated if they died. Bridge's family had already lost their patriarch and the eldest daughter. She couldn't bear it if they also lost the middle son.

Flames cracked and popped as they shot into the cabin just as a window broke and shattered into pieces. They were out of time. "We have to go under," she said. "Now."

Bridge lifted the old hatch and he went in first, helping Molly next. Now it was Wendy's turn but the opening was too small for her and the hefty crammed-full backpack. She shrugged out of it and passed it down, then crouched to climb down the ladder. Then she stopped.

"I'll be right there."

"Now, Wendy. We have no time," Bridge called.

He was right but who knew when they'd be able to find adequate shelter again. Molly needed protecting and she was worth the risk. Pieces of the roof rained down randomly and Wendy played a dangerous dodgeball game with fire. The east side of the cabin raged with flames and the black sooty smoke poured in. Dropping to her belly, she coughed as smoke entered her lungs, coating it like tar. Her eyes burned but she pushed through until she reached the bedroom, which was now in flames overhead. Someone must have doused the sides and roof with gasoline since Bridge's last perimeter sweep. Someone who knew how to be silent. Someone who had been watching and timing the intervals between Bridge's outdoor sweeps.

Only a person who had practice with slipping around silently, without being seen could do this. A phantom.

Archer Crow came to mind. He had access to information on Molly's whereabouts and he could move like wind. Never see him coming. Only knowing he had been there because of the devastation left.

But why hire Bridge then? The answer came swiftly. Surely he also knew about Wendy dating Bridge. He was a surefire way to force Wendy's hand. Whether she liked it or not, Bridge was a soft and tender spot for Wendy and always would be. She would come out of hiding to protect him.

This was why the CIA frowned on operatives having close connections and love interests. They made an agent weak. Emotional ties could and would be used as leverage and even blackmail, leaving an operative in a state of anxiety on every mission.

She'd loved too deeply. And it had cost her. Dearly.

Wendy grabbed the thermal sleeping bag, thankful she'd stocked up her backpack with batteries and water bottles after finding them. Working as a CIA operative meant never procrastinating. A second of idleness could mean death.

Hot debris rained down and she dodged them as they came too close for comfort. But she hadn't come this far to fail. She was going to make it to the trap door. Her lungs burned and itched, the smoke irritating and angering them.

Slow was smooth and smooth was fast. The mantra echoed in her mind.

The couch was covered in flames closer to the trap door than she liked. The flames were engulfing it and flaring over the hatch. It reminded her of jump roping as a kid.

Two girls swinging the rope while the jumper

timed it just right, then jumped in without missing a beat or tripping over the rope.

She was going to have to play it again, only this time it wasn't for fun. It was a fight for her life. If she mistimed her leap, she'd be caught on fire even though her coat was flame retardant. The rest of her was not.

She tossed the sleeping bag down the hatch and waited a beat or two, gathering her courage. Finally ready to act, she saw the flames from the couch were now too widespread for her to safely climb down the trap door.

Her only choice was to go out the front door and take her chances.

"I can't make it, Bridge," she yelled. "Take Molly and find a way out. I'll rendezvous one click south of here. Take a straight line."

She wasn't sure if he heard or if there was a way out. This could be the end of the road for all of them.

"Be—be careful. I care about you both!" It was the best she could do. All the time she had. She ran out the front door onto the porch and she rolled down the steps into the snow covered with ash, melted in places from the fire and heat. Jumping to her feet, she started running for the south side of the cabin. She had to make it 0.62 miles—one click. Keeping a keen eye on the snow for tracks or evidence of a laid trap, she plowed ahead, past the cabin and toward the woods. Snow reached her knees, making the trek slower than she'd anticipated or liked, but there was nothing she could do about it. Nothing she could do about the irritation of her lungs thanks to inhaling smoke either. It was hard to keep from coughing up a storm and giving away her position, but she focused on the mission and shut down every other thought just as she'd been trained to do when challenges and pain arose.

As she entered the woods, a brief sense of relief descended and she turned back to see the entire cabin engulfed in flames. She prayed Bridge and Molly would find a way out. When she turned, something heavy fell down on top of her, sending her to the ground in a heap and then a jolt of electricity ran through her body, incapacitating her.

She had been tased.

Below the cabin was a carved-out tunnel that might have been a bunker at one time. Who knew why it had been made and by whom. Conspiracy theorist. Homesteader. Serial killer. It was anybody's guess.

Bridge's muscles were tight and hearing Wendy's hollers of not being able to maneuver down the trap door had his nerves on edge. He'd tried to climb back up but the opening was covered in flames. Had she made it out? But if she had, she'd be directly in the path of her abductor.

Now he and Molly were following the underground tunnel to who knows where. It was damp and musty, packed-in hard earth, but it was surprisingly comfortable under here temperature-wise. He had Molly moving ahead of him and the LED battery-operated lantern from Wendy's backpack gave them light. Cobwebs and critters were down here but Molly didn't seem to mind.

"Is Nanny Wendy going to die?"

"No. She's trained in combat. She's smart and sharp so she'll be able to take care of herself." He was mostly reminding himself of her attributes to convince himself she would be okay. In a click south, they'd be together again and head down this sinister mountain. If he never saw another mountain again, it would be too soon.

"If bad people are trying to kill her and the elements are dangerous, how can you be sure?"

She was worried for Wendy even if her words came out monotone and her face was expressionless.

Molly worked in facts, science and numbers so he answered in kind. "She's ninety-nine-point-nine percent safe." He couldn't lie. Molly wouldn't buy it. She wasn't the kind of kid who would believe you if the facts didn't line up accurately. He admired it and was amused by it. But it made reassuring her a lot harder.

She didn't respond to his percentage so Bridge wasn't sure if it comforted her or not. He wasn't comforted in the least. If Wendy had made it out, she was alone in the elements.

Someone had sneaked by him to pour accelerant on the cabin and set it ablaze. This happened on his watch and he'd failed.

Just like he'd failed little Levi James and his FBI colleague he'd trained, Roy Rickman. He could not handle another death on his watch and certainly not Wendy's. Bridge couldn't deny he'd often wondered if Wendy had died in these past three years, but deep down he refused to believe that. She was skilled and trained. But he knew that didn't make her invincible. And now the idea that she could be dead in the cabin or out there in the snow sickened him.

A world without Wendy Dawson was a world no one should have to wade through. She made it brighter. Always had.

Whoever had pulled this fire stunt was definitely a pro. Maybe not even someone on the dark web payroll but one of Anderson Crawley's assassins. Former CIA or present. Possible black ops. Former military. A formidable opponent against Wendy.

Adrenaline kicked in and Bridge itched to

gain the freedom to find her. But he also had Molly to look out for. He couldn't leave her alone for a long period of time. If men on the mountain didn't hurt her, there were enough natural oppositions and deadly animals that could harm or kill her.

His hands were tied but his prayers were not and he spent the next few moments interceding on Wendy's behalf. The tunnel was a straight shot, but to where he wasn't sure. He plowed ahead, urging on Molly, but in minutes they came to a dead end.

No!

Then he spotted the old rusty ladder that ran from the floor to above their heads. A way out. He nearly cried with relief. "Okay, Molly, I'm going to climb up and see what's around us and make sure it's safe, then up you'll go and I'll be right behind you. Hang tight."

"I cannot hang tight when my feet are on the floor. Gravity keeps me from hanging and what exactly does *hang tight* mean?" She looked at him with inquisitive eyes and an honest expression.

"It means stay here and don't go anywhere. Be patient until I return."

"Then you should just say that."

"You're right." When would he learn to say exactly what he meant around her? It would definitely save him time in these situations. He pulled on the ladder to test its durability and when he found it was sturdy enough to hold his frame, he climbed up and pushed on the make-shift door. It wasn't locked but it was heavy with snow and anything else that was covering it. Could be a branch or boulder.

He'd been working out a lot since Wendy left. His way to burn off feeling and emotion and to some degree a fair amount of anxiety as he worried over her every single day, knowing her career and how deadly it could be. He pushed on the door a few times, feeling it budge, then it finally broke free and the wind barreled into the tunnel. Light had peeped over the horizon, but the skies were still gray and bloated. No pretty pinks or purples to paint the morning. He missed Texas sunrises.

But the snow had stopped and he was thankful for that and also not. It had been a great camouflage when they were exposed and vulnerable. He surveyed the area. The wind had formed snowdrifts and it appeared like it had snowed longer and harder than it had.

"Molly, I need to go and check on Nanny Wendy. But it's dangerous for you. Down here, you're safe. Are you going to be okay if I leave you down here and come back for you?"

"Can I have a lantern?"

"Absolutely." He handed her Wendy's backpack. "Inside is granola bars, water and batteries. Also toilet paper if you need to find a spot in the tunnel. You may do what you need to. But don't leave the tunnel. Stay down here and I'll return for you. Or Nanny Wendy will. But only the two of us. It might take a little time but don't be concerned. Okay?"

She nodded and dug into the backpack retrieving a chocolate chip granola bar and a bottle of water. He didn't want to leave her but she was safer here than anywhere else and it wasn't so cold she'd perish or become frostbitten. He climbed up the ladder and onto the mountain, then he closed the hatch and shoved snow over the top. He also ripped a sliver of his shirt, tied it to a stick and staked it in the snow to help him remember where she was. Not that he'd forget, and he had the tracker in his watch to keep tabs, but it never hurt if something happened to him and it was up to Wendy to find her.

He was going to leave footprints in the snow and without fresh snow to cover them, any tracker would see footprints coming out of nowhere. He used a branch to mask them, but there was no way to hide someone had been here. He could only pray and hope Molly wouldn't be found. No one might want to kill her but she'd make great leverage in forcing Wendy to give herself up. She would die for that little girl. And so would Bridge. She'd grown on him since providing protective detail for her.

He hunched forward, facing the brutal wind, and jogged back toward the cabin, pushing through the snow and feeling the burn in his legs. But he welcomed it. It meant he was alive. About half a click ahead, he spotted a figure dressed in camouflage and carrying something.

Not something.

Someone.

Wendy!

If he fired a warning shot, the guy might do something drastic. He hated second-guessing himself but after the fiasco when he worked for the CIRG, he hadn't been the same. Taking this job was a mistake.

His gut said give chase. A gunshot would speed the assailant up and Bridge had a chasm of distance between them. The abductor wasn't moving at a fast pace. Was she dead? No, they needed her alive. She must be incapacitated and unconscious, otherwise Wendy would be giving him the fight of her life and that would prove deadly for him. She was a human weapon.

Keeping to the trees for shelter, Bridge continued his approach.

Someone else sprang from the shadows dressed in all black, including a face covering.

He was too large and wide to be a woman. The man carrying Wendy pulled a gun and fired at the black-clad man but missed and the second guy fired back. Bridge feared that in the exchange of bullets Wendy might end up hit.

Bridge would give anything for a rifle. Anything to set the sights and pick them both off to protect Wendy, but he had only a handgun and with the wind, he might not even be a crack shot. He'd use the distraction to his advantage. The abductor dropped Wendy and took cover but nearby as the other shooter dodged into the trees as well, disappearing.

A few moments later Wendy fidgeted with her constraints as the first shooter disappeared and reappeared behind the second shooter. They engaged in combat, and that gave Bridge a chance to rescue Wendy.

He sneaked along the edge of the forest, avoiding the fight ensuing and let out the whistle he'd been using to communicate. The raspy, buzzing whistle of the purple finch, native to these mountains. Wendy's head perked up. Her arms were constrained behind her back and she worked to find something in her boot pocket, probably a knife.

As the men rolled in the snow, Bridge took his chance and raced to Wendy. He'd already pulled his army knife. He slit the zip ties on her hands and then her feet.

She sprang up and they darted into the woods while the two idiots continued to fight, leaving the whole point of their struggle unattended. Which meant they might not know Wendy had been with anyone else. That gave them an edge.

"What happened?" he asked her when they were hidden by trees.

"I got tased by that elephant and then zip-tied. Whatever voltage he was using was tough. Where's Molly?" Wendy asked. She was winded but her eyes were narrowed and fuming. She was mad that someone got the jump on her.

"She's safe. I left her in the tunnel, which turned out to be a straight shot to your suggested rendezvous point. She has supplies and a lantern. I think she'll be as okay as a ten-year-old girl on the run can be." Not saying a lot.

"Good. When they realize I've vanished, they'll track me—or at the very least one of them will. For that kind of money I suspect a fight to the death unless one of them escapes."

"Agreed," Bridge said.

"Once we make it off this mountain and to Bear Valley, we can take down Anderson but it won't be easy."

"We can have my team in wait, ready to spring into action."

He followed Wendy as they jogged through the forest, pushing through the snow on their way to Molly. "Well, we can discuss it later."

She didn't want to use his team at all. When would she trust him? No one on his team would double-cross them. They could not be bought. Instead of sniping back, he let it go. For now. "Right now, we have to make it off this mountain in one piece and get to civilization."

She agreed and they made their way back to the tunnel. Bridge lifted the hatch and called down. "Molly, it's Bridge and Nanny Wendy. We're coming down."

"Okay. I ate a granola bar and drank a bottle of water."

Bridge climbed down and Wendy followed. "I'd say let's take a beat but once those guys realize I'm gone, they're going to follow the tracks right here. We need to be long gone."

Except their footprints would be tracked out of here too. They could use a branch with twigs and leaves but a good tracker would know the technique. "Then let's get going. Molly, you ready?"

"I want to go home." She didn't whine, merely stated a fact.

"I know," Wendy said. "We'll have you back to your uncle and safe as soon as we can."

Without another word Wendy climbed out,

Molly next and then Bridge. Disappearing into the trees, they headed down the mountain.

"Do you hear that?" Molly asked.

They paused and Bridge heard it. A buzzing sound. "That's a drone."

What he didn't know was if it had only a camera or was weaponized.

A bullet hit a nearby tree, splintering bark and giving him an answer.

"Run!"

NINE

Someone with serious tech-savvy skills and money was operating this weaponized drone and could be miles away. "We got a predator drone, Bridge." The craft was locked and loaded and they were in its sights. "Probably going to try and injure me, take you out so the operator can then retrieve me. I'm a lot easier to catch if I'm wounded."

Wendy felt like a little rabbit being chased by a wolf with a hungry belly and sharp fangs. Her stomach twisted into knots as her adrenaline spiked. "We have to separate."

"No way," Bridge said as they ducked into a denser area of the forest, using treetops as coverage. Another bullet fired and hit about a foot away from Bridge. As Wendy suspected, the operator was working to deactivate Bridge, wound her and then extract her for relocation.

Not happening.

She argued her point again. "If I run into thick

foliage, the drone will have to drop in order to spot me. That will give you time to shoot it down."

His hardened jaw and narrowed eyes revealed he wasn't into the plan but they had no other choice. From the sound and the accuracy, she could tell the drone was shooting a rifle. She wished he had one of those.

"Molly," Bridge said, "we need you to stay crouched down right here in this thicket." He helped her maneuver into it. "You stay here until you hear me whistle. I'll do it four times so you know it's me and not a bird. Do you understand?"

"What's not to understand? You're leading a drone with a gun away, and when it's safe, you'll whistle four times like a bird."

Bridge smirked, but his jaw was still hardened. "Exactly that."

Molly got into position.

Wendy's heart beat roughly against her chest. "And I'm off with a wing and a prayer." She darted toward a thick tree line as bullets rained down but she kept her eye on the prize and her prayers going up and out for God to be her shield. Snow sprayed all around her feet. When the gun was out of bullets, the operator would have to bring it back unless he'd built something like the Israeli army with a clip changer.

Once she was inside the thick trees, tight and dense, she waited in hopes the drone would lower in order to cut through the foliage to see its target. Once it was lower, Bridge could lock in and blow it to smithereens. She had full confidence in Bridge's skill. He'd been shooting tin cans off fence posts since he was five. He had 20/20 vision and was a crack shot. Now to be the bait. She came out of her crouch, darting into a sparse set of trees.

Another shot hit the ground right next to her foot. Entirely too close for comfort. She dove into a snowy bramble, watching from the spaces between gnarled branches. The drone lowered.

Dropped again.

That's it. Come on, baby, just a little...more...

Gunfire erupted and the drone fell to the forest floor. Bridge had done it. "Yes," she whispered and broke free from the bushes, running down the drone. She unlatched the rifle and the extra cartridges. This was highly sophisticated and military grade. Not good. But for now she had what she needed. She used the rifle to smash the drone into as many pieces as she could, then slung the gun on her back and jogged back to the bush where Molly hid.

Bridge emerged seconds later with a grin on his face. "I'm not saying I'm a bad shot. I'm saying I'm an excellent shot."

"And humble about it too."

"He's not being humble, Nanny Wendy. He's being arrogant."

"I'm being a jokester," Bridge said. "I'm joking."

"I don't get it." Molly brushed snow from her pants and looked at Wendy. "I'm thirsty and hungry."

Wendy dug into her backpack for a bottle of water, then handed it to Molly. She gave one to Bridge who drank sparingly. Wendy did the same. She had several bottles but the people after her weren't making her trek down the mountain easy or quick. What should have been a few hours was proving to be more like days.

After Molly finished an entire bottle, Wendy handed her another granola bar and put the empty bottle in the backpack. They began their descent, walking in silence. Bloated gray skies revealed more snow on the way or possible rain. She hoped the former. Rain would be disastrous right now. They were already cold and to add water meant ice later when the temperature dropped overnight. The last thing she wanted was hypothermia setting in.

"Looks like some weather is moving in again," Wendy said. "We need to find a river. If we find one, we might find a fishing shack."

Bridge blew out a heavy breath. "I'd like a

break. Just one little break. The weather to be on our side for once."

"Weather can't be on a side." Molly marched like a trooper, though she was already slowing some.

"You're right," Bridge said. His patience to handle what could be irksome was admirable. Wendy always knew he'd be a good father. This was proof and it sent a flutter through her middle.

"What do you like to study most?" he asked.

"I like dogs. I know every breed of dog alphabetically."

"Oh fun," he said and tossed an amused glance to Wendy. "Okay, Molly, give us all the dog breeds in alphabetical order."

"Affenpinscher, Afghan hound, Airedale terrier, Akita, Alaskan Klee Kai…"

"What's an Alaskan Klee Kai?" Bridge asked, genuinely interested.

"It's a relatively new breed of dog that's similar to but smaller than the husky. The name *Klee Kai* comes from an Inuit term meaning *small dog.*"

Bridge held up a branch for Molly to walk under, then kept it up for Wendy too. She passed by him and mouthed, "Thank you for keeping her entertained."

"I'm the one entertained," he muttered under

his breath and Wendy snickered. He turned to Molly. "So you don't just know the names in alphabetical order but you know about each breed too."

"Oh yes," she said with more enthusiasm than Wendy had heard since she found her at the horse camp. "You want me to finish?"

"Have at it, kid."

"Alaskan malamute, American bulldog, American cocker spaniel, American Eskimo dog..."

"Do you have a favorite dog?" Bridge interrupted when she hit the dogs that started with the letter D.

"I like the Shetland sheepdog. People think it's a small collie but it's its own breed. Bred for sheepherding in the Shetland terrain. They're sweet little dogs and so smart and they're very soft. My friend Ranjana had one that was black, tan and white. His name was Mohan."

"I could use a good herding dog. I live on a ranch and we have horses and we now have sheep thanks to Miss Emily who is married to my older brother, Stone."

"Stone is a rock."

"Yeah, a real hardhead."

Wendy laughed at Bridge's joke. Bridge might not be named after a rock, but was as hardheaded as they came. She also admired that. Until it was in opposition with her. Then they were like billy goats locking horns.

"That doesn't make sense, Bridge," Molly said.

"Never mind. Okay, we were on Dandie Dinmont terrier," he said, cueing her in to continue her list.

"Deerhound, Doberman, Dogue De Bordeaux…"

Bridge turned and made a dramatic display of an eye roll and Wendy laughed under her breath. "Dogue de Bordeaux. Fancy," Wendy said.

"It's not fancy, Nanny Wendy. It's just a French mastiff."

"Oh. Keep going."

And she did which kept them all busy and focused on something other than the fact abductors and killers were lurking and any moment danger could spring up like a creepy clown in a jack-in-the-box. Not to mention it was bitter cold and Molly's nose was running. She hoped the child wasn't coming down with something. Now was not the time for any of them to be sick.

Bridge paused up ahead and pivoted. "You hear that?"

Wendy listened. Wind in the trees. Snaps. Cracks.

And water. They'd found the river.

"Nice," she said. "Be on the lookout for a fishing shack." As she said the words, a dot of rain plopped right onto her nose. "And let's look fast. It's about to pour down."

The sky had turned an inky black like a chemical fire had been set off in the atmosphere and in the distance thunder belched. Sounds of rushing water grew louder as they approached the snowy banks of the river.

"Hey!" Bridge called her attention to a small but sturdy little shanty. It wasn't cozy but it was going to keep them dry until the rain passed, which she hoped was soon. They didn't have enough food to keep them going for another day or two. "Let's go."

"Wait. We have to be cautious. What if one of them spotted it too? What if they're using it to wait for us?" What if the gunmen on their tail found them inside and it was set on fire? Not every cabin or shack came with its own underground tunnel.

Wendy put the rifle scope from the drone to her eye and used it to survey the perimeter. Everything appeared safe but that might be just what the people hired to extract her would want them to think. But the rain poured down faster. No more waiting around. "Okay let's go."

They darted around the banks to the old fishing shack and walked right inside. It was smaller than the cabin. No kitchen but there was a gas cooking grill, a few outdoor chairs, two cots on each wall and a wood-burning stove with a little firewood stacked beside it. The floor was old and wooden and the place needed repairs and an air freshener. The evidence of critters littered the old floor and one of the cots, but the roof was solid and that's really all they needed—a dry place to wait out the rain.

With some old rags lying in a heap, Wendy dusted off the cots while Bridge went to work building a fire. Molly had paused on the T dog names and was sitting in a chair with her fidget spinner. "Nanny Wendy, do you want me to continue with the alphabetical dog names?"

"Do you want to?"

"Yes. I don't like not finishing what I started," she said quietly.

Bridge snorted and closed the wood-burning stove.

"And what's with that little remark?" Wendy asked, already her ire rising.

"Nothing." He brushed by her and she grabbed his arm. He looked at her hold, then at her. "Let go of my arm."

"What does that mean?" she asked as Molly was on toy fox terrier.

"It just means you didn't follow through on us. I thought with how intelligent you were, you'd have picked up the context clue."

Wendy dropped his arm, feeling stung. "I was protecting you. I'm still protecting you. Remember *that*." She could stomp off but there was nowhere to go but outside. And it was pouring. The roof wasn't that thick and the rain was like pounding fists on the tin.

"I can protect myself. I could have helped protect you."

"Welsh terrier, West Highland white terrier, Westiepoo, whippet…" Molly droned on, oblivious to their heated tiff.

"And have your mom go out to her car one day and get blown up?"

Bridge's eyes narrowed. "Well, seeing how she's had cancer, she's not really up to driving her car so…"

Wendy's blood froze and her mouth dropped open. "What? What kind of cancer? How long?" Wendy had loved Marisol Spencer. Bridge's mother had welcomed her with open arms and been like a mother to her, especially since she had no parents. Tears welled in her eyes. "How bad…?"

Bridge's eyes softened and he sighed. "I'm sorry. That was a rotten thing to do to you. I didn't tell you last night when we talked about the family because I knew it would upset you. She's not technically cancer-free but her last scan was clean so she's good for another six months.

It's been hard but she's been a champ. Having the grandbabies has helped, and Stone and Emily live on the ranch and take good care of her."

Wendy walked to the door and turned her back to Bridge as tears fell down her cheeks. If Anderson hadn't burned her and her life had gone according to plan, she could have been there to see to Marisol's needs, take her to doctor appointments, cook meals and keep her company during chemo treatments. She'd lost so much. Bridge was angry and that was fair, but he didn't seem to realize how much she'd lost. How much she'd suffered.

The tears wouldn't stop and this was so unlike Wendy. She wasn't a crier. She was a pull-your-self-up-by-your-bootstraps-and-live-to-fight-another-day kind of woman. But Marisol had been sick and she'd never known. What if she had died?

Large warm hands held her shoulders. "Wendy," Bridge murmured. "Please forgive me. I shouldn't have used my sick mom, of all things, to hurt you. I shouldn't be doing anything to hurt you. I promised you once that I would never intentionally do that and here I am going back on my word. I'm so sorry." He turned her around and drew her to his chest and she let him.

She had no fight left. Wrapping her arms around his waist, she cried into his shirt. "I didn't want to leave Bridge. I wanted to stay, to marry you, have children. Be a family, have a family. For once. I've been through things. Dark things."

He stroked her hair, something she'd always loved; the act had soothed her every time when she was keyed up. She loved his scent and his strong arms. How could arms this powerful be this tender at the same time?

"When I found the fourth piece of code, I was captured in Tokyo and taken to a North Korean prison, but I stashed the flash drive before they found it. I went back for it after I escaped. I spent six months there, Bridge. You think I wanted that? That I wasn't thinking of you every single day and what our life could have been? I didn't want to hurt you but the whole family was in danger at Anderson's—and other enemies'—hands. I had to cut all ties. I've been alone. Just me. Well, me and God."

Bridge raised her chin, wiped away her tears with the pads of his thumbs. "I'm so sorry, Wendy. I've been so angry and hurt that I never thought how these years have affected you. If you want to talk about what happened, I'll listen."

Another thing Wendy had loved about Bridge. But she didn't want to talk about imprisonment or torture or lack of sleep or food or unsanitary conditions. "I appreciate that. For now, I just want off this mountain, to quit fighting and bickering with you and to keep Molly safe."

Bridge kicked himself at how steely he'd been. Wendy had been held captive for a period of time, and he couldn't begin to imagine the horrors she'd experienced. He didn't blame her for not wanting to talk about it and now wasn't the setting anyway. Little ears were nearby, and while she might appear to be unobservant, Molly Wingbender was a smart cookie with a wildly keen mind. But she was still just a child who didn't need to hear grown-up conversations.

"I agree, Wendy," he said. "Right now that's all we can do." He lowered his hands to his sides. "You know, I can't imagine my company doesn't have drones of their own flying around on the mountain searching for us."

"They might."

When Bridge didn't check in, they'd go on a high alert and when they discovered Molly missing, it would be all-hands-on-deck. All spyware and technology enlisted to scour the area for them. So far it was a bust though. They needed off this mountain and then a game plan.

Briefly they'd discussed running a ruse to get the rendezvous point but by now, surely, Anderson Crawley knew she wasn't working alone.

Someone might have asked for more money since another man was involved—Bridge. Who knows how Anderson knew all the things he did, but he did.

Rain poured like buckets, eating away snow and leaving puddles on the porch thanks to the wind. Bridge was over the weather. Cold and snow and rain. When he was back in Texas, and this case was over, he was heading to a sandy beach with lava-like temperatures and a delicious fruity drink filled with coconut and pineapple. That sounded like a dream right now compared to pewter skies and torrential rain and now dirty mush instead of pristine white snow.

The shack warmed up quickly and Wendy began pilfering through a Rubbermaid cabinet, putting anything that might be of use into the backpacks. Molly sat on a cot toying with a necklace she wore. First time he'd even noticed the child wearing jewelry. "Whatcha got on, Molly?"

"A necklace."

He should have known that answer was coming. One had to be direct and precise if he wanted a direct and precise answer. Molly didn't do small talk or casual conversation and he actually liked that about her as he wasn't big on either himself. "What is the shape?"

"It's a heart-shaped locket. But it doesn't open so it's not really a locket. My dad called it that."

"He gave it to you?"

"It was my mother's. She gave it to me."

"That was nice." Kind of a weird gift for a baby. But Molly probably didn't wear it until she was old enough not to swallow or choke on it. He wasn't exactly sure what age that would be. His younger brother, Rhode, swallowed a nickel when he was fourteen, so...

"It was nice. Giving gifts is always a nice gesture. My dad gave me a laptop before he died. It was yellow like a school bus."

Bridge sat on a lawn chair and opened a bottle of water. "Do you miss horse camp?"

"I like horses. I liked horse camp. You're a good teacher." She continued to toy with the locket, then she tucked it under her shirt and retrieved her fidget spinner.

"Thank you. You're a good student."

"I know." He loved how she acknowledged facts without arrogance. Just sweet and childlike.

The rain was finally easing up and fish might be biting. He noticed some fishing gear. Rods and reels. Line and a tackle box of bait. Might as well attempt to make himself useful. "I'm going to see about catching some fish for dinner. We could use that gas camping grill."

Wendy held a roll of gauze in one hand and

fishing line in the other. "Sounds good. Anything with protein would be amazing." She shoved the supplies into her backpack and closed the cabinet door. "You want any help?"

"Nah. I could use the alone time to be honest."

She swallowed and nodded. "Right. I understand. I hope you have success."

"Me too." He carried the fishing gear outside. The wind was cold and the air damp, the smell of earth and fish rolling off the river. As he worked on baiting the hook, it brought back memories of his father teaching him and his brothers how to fish. One day he wanted a family and children he could teach too. Didn't have to be boys to teach it to. Not all boys liked to fish. Some girls loved it. It was always about the person. Often Rhode had stayed home to be with their mom while he and Stone went fishing with Dad. Never bothered Dad or Mom.

"Bridge?"

Bridge turned to find Molly standing a few feet away. "I would like to try to fish if that would be acceptable?"

His heart warmed. It was like God knew he needed this. "It would be acceptable." No point getting all gooey with Molly about it. She wasn't gooey, and would likely not respond to sentiment the way he had. Although she was toying with her locket, which could mean Molly was homesick, curious or sad about missing her mom and dad. Or it might simply be another outlet for self-soothing when she didn't want to use her fidget spinner.

"We're going to fish for bass," he told her.

"Bass means the common European freshwater perch or any of a number of fish similar to or related to the perch. I read that in the Oxford Languages dictionary."

"I had no idea that's where you read it," he teased, knowing Molly wouldn't pick up on the humor. Still he marveled at her ability to recall everything she read. The kid was remarkable.

"Yes. I know the entire dictionary and Webster's too. I like to cite the Oxford more often though."

"Yeah, me too," he joked again but she didn't notice. "Have you ever fished?"

"No, but I've seen videos of men fishing."

"Well, this particular spinner bait, which is what we're going to use first, is a great choice to catch bass. Let me show you how to cast." He showed her how to press and hold down the button on the back of the reel, then rear back behind and release the button as he cast the line onto the water. "From here we're going to slowly turn the reel crank and wait for a bite."

"How do you know you have a bite?" she asked.

"Great question. You'll feel a tug and you'll see the lure bob. Then you'll reel that sucker in."

"We're not catching suckers, Bridge. We're catching fish. You buy suckers. Although you can buy fish at the market too." She peered up at him with her big doe eyes.

He couldn't help but grin. "You're right. I'll go first and show you how and then you can try. Hopefully they'll bite." It wasn't exactly fishing season but with the rain they might be biting. He was hoping and praying.

He cast three times before he felt the tug on his line. "I got a bite, Molly. You see the bob in the water?"

"I do." Her inflection didn't change but she was observing with more care and her hands stimmed at her sides. She was excited.

Bridge reeled in a nice-sized bass. "Look at that, Molly! What do you think?"

She only nodded.

Bridge unhooked it and dropped it in a bucket of river water. "Your turn. You ready?"

She nodded again. He walked her through the actions again and then handed her the rod and reel. For a first try, Molly did well and slowly began reeling.

"Nice job, Molly."

"I don't feel a tug yet."

"It might take a few—"

The lure bobbed and Molly looked at Bridge. "I felt a tug."

"You've got one! Slowly pull and reel it in." He knelt beside her, encouraging her as she reeled in the line and pulled the fish up out of the water. A very nice-sized bass. "Wow that's bigger than the one I caught. Your first fish. Here, hold it up and I'll take a picture." He might not have internet or Wi-Fi, but he could snap a photo. Every fisherman or woman needed a picture of their first catch. "Smile."

She did, though it was a little forced, and he snapped the photo. "Okay. I'll help unhook him. They can wiggle some."

"I caught my first fish."

"You certainly did." Bridge beamed and now Molly was smiling. "Was it fun?"

She nodded.

"You want to try again?"

Another nod. After a few more casts Molly caught her second fish and it was a whopper. They had plenty of food for tonight so there was no point in continuing. These fish would give them the protein they needed for strength to finish the hike down the mountain and into the nearest town.

When Bridge turned around, Wendy stood on the little porch with her arms folded over her chest and a smile filling her face. Guess she'd watched the whole thing. "It's cold out," she told Molly. "Your nose is still running too. Why don't you go inside and I'll be in shortly."

"Okay. Thank you, Bridge. I like fishing."

"Me too, Molly." She darted up the yard into the fishing shack and Wendy made her way down to the banks.

"That was sweet of you."

"She asked. She's a natural. Wish I could take her out in a boat. She would love fishing off a boat. I always did."

"You're a good teacher. Probably why they picked you as an instructor in the Critical Incident Response Group. You have an easy way of explaining things."

He caught the admiration in her eyes and it swelled his chest. He'd always wanted to make Wendy proud. Wanted her respect and appreciation. If she knew the blunder in Atlanta that had caused the death of an agent and child, she might not admire him so much.

She cocked her head. "What is it?"

"How after this long can you still read my thoughts or mannerisms?"

"One, I know you. Two, it's part of my job." She smirked and he laughed.

"Good point." Why did he care what she thought or didn't think of him? They weren't a couple, and even if they'd had a moment earlier and could empathize with one another, it didn't make up for her abandoning him. Even if it was to protect him. But out here on the run he found he wanted to actually talk about what happened in Atlanta. He ignored the fact it was with her. That might mean something he wasn't ready to consider. "I took a recruit I'd trained down to Atlanta undercover in a child-trafficking ring. I'd mentioned we'd been investigating it before Christmas." Before she left him.

"I remember that."

"A boy had been taken from a day care by a family friend who was involved. He was on the pickup list, which in itself is tragic. To trust someone only to be betrayed by them…"

She shifted.

"I wasn't taking a shot at you."

She sniffed. "I know. But it felt like one because I know that's how you feel about me."

He ignored that. She wasn't wrong. "We went in as buyers. Long story short, it went sideways and the recruit I brought in was killed and Levi James, the little boy, was hit by accident on our way out. Both of them died when it should have been me. I shouldn't have let my recruit do his first extraction so soon. He needed more time."

"Bridge, if you put him in, then it's because you thought he was ready. You're a thorough instructor and a good teacher with a keen eye for candidates. You're feeling guilty—and a measure of survivor's guilt too, which is normal—but it was not your fault. It was a horrible tragedy because horrible people created that dangerous environment. Every agent going in knows the dangers, the possible loss of life to protect citizens. He knew that."

She wasn't saying anything he hadn't already told himself, then ignored. But hearing it come from her meant something more to him. Wendy was a straight shooter.

"Sometimes our jobs go sideways. Evil doesn't fight fair, Bridge. Never has. Never will. Evil fights dirty and hasn't a single ounce of mercy. We get caught in direct fire and sometimes cross fire and then it keeps on coming while trying to make us feel guilty. To make us feel like this wicked cruel war is our fault, like it originated with us. Don't let it win by keeping you down and defeated. You're a fighter. Keep fighting the good fight."

He had let the enemy pummel him and keep on doing it. It was time to say enough but that was easier said than done. He rarely got a single night's rest without a nightmare about that night. About Roy's wife crying and Levi's family huddled and sobbing, but thanking him that he'd at least tried to get the boy out. According to the family, God had spared the child from all that happened to young children in these kinds of trafficking rings. But dead didn't seem spared to Bridge.

"Thank you for those words, Wendy. I needed to hear them. Now I need to believe them. That's harder than simply hearing them."

"I know. It's easier for me to say them to you than to myself about situations I've been in. Isn't it funny how we have such big faith for others but pretty much none when it comes to ourselves?"

"Molly would say that it is not funny."

Wendy chuckled. "She would. But you know what I mean."

"I do. And I think I've had enough heart-to-heart for now. I'll work on fileting the fish for dinner instead." He headed back out to the bucket and used a filet knife in the shack to debone and filet the fish, then he dumped the rest in the river and let it wash downstream. Didn't need bears or mountain lions sniffing out food. Once inside, Wendy had the grill fired up and Molly was on her cot with the fidget spinner.

"I found some salt and pepper in the cabinet." Wendy handed it to him and he went to work grilling the several filets. They ate them off paper towels, devouring each bite and savoring every morsel. When their bellies were full, Wendy covered Molly with a blanket and told her to try to sleep. She didn't put up a fight about it.

Bridge wasn't going to either. "You want first or second watch?"

"I'll take first watch. You caught the food so you deserve to sleep first." She put on her coat and slung the rifle over her arm. "We need to break camp at first light. I'll wake you around two a.m. and catch three hours myself."

"I'm not going to fight you on it. I'm exhausted."

Wendy patted his shoulder. "I'll keep you safe."

He had no doubt. He curled up on the dusty cot and closed his eyes. He must have gone into a coma or something because when he woke, it was almost light.

Why hadn't Wendy woken him for his shift?

Where was she?

TEN

Bridge jumped up and grabbed his coat and gun as he raced outside, panic building in his chest and tightening it with vise-like force. No more snow had fallen and no more rain. This worked in his favor as he searched for tracks. He retraced their steps down to the river and then from there he saw Wendy's tracks up on the east side of the shack, as if she'd been doing a sweep. He ran up the trail and followed them to the back of the house where there were two sets of prints now. One much larger. A man. The prints were mixed together, overlapping. A struggle had ensued.

Wendy had been taken.

It had to have been by someone as skilled or more skilled than she was. He'd have to track her and pray no more snow fell or they'd lose the prints. Darting back inside, he collected the backpacks and woke Molly. How was he going to tell her Nanny Wendy was missing? She already knew they were being chased by men out to harm them. Molly needed the truth. She lived in the realm of absolute truths, facts and science. He lightly shook her awake. "Hey, Molly, we have to go right now. Nanny Wendy's been taken but we can track the footprints and rescue her. I know she's alive and safe enough."

Molly sat up ramrod straight. "Okay, Bridge. If anyone can find her and rescue her, I know it's you. You're very good at protecting us."

The backs of Bridge's eyes burned. Out of the mouths of babes. The words came from the most honest person he'd ever met. God knew he needed to hear it. "Thank you. I'll do my best but I'm just a man and men aren't perfect."

"I know." She hopped off the bed and asked for toilet paper, then disappeared for a few seconds before returning, then once they had on their coats and supplies, they set out.

The temperatures were rising since the blizzard was over but it remained pretty cold. Molly's nose was still running and he'd noticed her coughing a few times. "Molly, do you feel sick?"

"I'm tired and my nose is itchy and my throat is irritated." Not a tickle or scratchy. Clinical.

"When we get to a town, we'll see about getting you to a doctor." Sounded like the common cold but he wasn't going to chance it.

Bridge followed the double tracks into the

woods for the first twenty feet. Then the tracks changed to a single set of prints. Her abductor must have knocked her out, but not for long because the double prints appeared again. He was forcing her to walk. But where? The rendezvous point? Surely he'd taken a video to prove she was alive in order to obtain the drop-off location and then get his reward money.

If she was alert and away from camp, then why not fight back? What would keep her walking with him—or her?

It had to do with Bridge and Molly and their safety. She was doing all over again what she'd done three years ago, proving that she was and always had been and always would be the lone wolf.

Anger boiled his blood, leaving him fuming and sweating. Anything could go wrong on this mission. What if the captor did something to her? They were to deliver her alive, but unharmed wasn't in the fine print. And what if it wasn't one person but more than one, who'd teamed up and planned to split the money? She might be outmanned. Though he had full confidence she could take down more than one person at a time if needed.

The footprints tracked along the river and the sound of rushing water whooshed in his ears as wind rustled the trees. "How are you doing, Molly?"

"I'm doing well. When we get to town, can I have a cheeseburger with bacon but no onions or tomato?"

"You absolutely can. I'm going to have one too." He kept his voice light and easy so as not to worry her. Inside he was a complete basket case. He could move so much faster without little feet slowing him down. His heart wanted to gallop ahead and race to rescue Wendy. But he had to keep his pace with Molly's.

The tracks thankfully led them down the mountain. The incline evened out more and because these hunters were after Wendy, no one was firing at him and Molly. At least for now. They weren't out of the woods, literally or metaphorically, yet. He could still be seen as a threat that needed to be removed so he kept a watchful eye on the woods. Bridge was taking no chances.

The tracks continued, only two sets, winding through the trees. The clouds had turned gray and hazy, and snow was falling again. No. He'd lose the tracks. Why couldn't they seem to catch a break?

Up ahead he heard movement. He quickly turned to Molly. "I need you to be still. Make no movement or sound. I think Nanny Wendy is up ahead." He put his index finger to his mouth. "Do you understand?"

Molly nodded and Bridge scanned his surroundings. About ten feet to the east was an old hollowed-out log. "Come on," he whispered and guided her to the log, thankful he hadn't made the promise she'd never have to take up homestead in one again, or this conversation wouldn't go as well as he hoped it would now. "I need you to crawl inside here. I know it's smelly and probably cold and wet but I need to hide you while I help Nanny Wendy. Can you be brave for me?"

"I can," she whispered and held her nose as she crawled into the hollowed-out log. "I don't like it in here."

"I know, Molly. I know. But you'll be safe there. Don't come out no matter what you hear. Me or Nanny Wendy will come back for you. Recite the dogs in alphabetical order inside your head and then do it again and again until we get back."

"Okay. Bridge, I know you'll find her and bring her back. You're a hero. Like Spider-Man except he's not real. No one can be bitten by a radioactive spider and shoot webs."

He grinned and was happy she had confidence in him. He didn't want to disappoint her. "You're right. They can't. Be small and still."

"I can only be as small as I actually am."

He opened his mouth to reply, then thought better. Now wasn't the time to explain and debate. "I'll be back. Or Nanny Wendy will." They couldn't both perish or Molly would be doomed out here and the thought sickened him. Once Molly was secure in the trunk and he couldn't see her from a distance, he rushed back to where he'd heard movement.

One man talked, but Bridge was pretty sure it wasn't directed to Wendy. Did he have a satellite phone? Bridge could use that to call his team. He gauged the situation, assessing from what angle he needed to attack. He climbed a tree to look over and out. A burly man in ski gear stood over Wendy with a satellite phone in hand. Had he gotten the rendezvous point yet?

He looked to Wendy. Her eye was black and almost swollen shut. He'd hit her. Bridge's blood ran so hot he might implode. How dare the man hurt her.

Wendy sat silently, her hands behind her back, but Bridge spotted movement and an object in her hand. A small knife. With ease Wendy freed herself. She must have stashed that knife within reach before she'd been taken. That meant she had willingly let this brute abduct her. Why? Because she wanted that rendezvous location in order to blitz Anderson and set her reputation right. But she still needed to put the pieces of code together and find someone who could erase the deepfake and reveal the true killer. That was the only way she could prove this was all done at Anderson Crawley's hands.

Now that he likely knew Wendy's plan—though he fumed she'd done it on her own again without allowing Bridge to be privy to it—he couldn't attack or shoot the man until he'd established proof-of-life and received the drop location. Bridge needed to move closer in order to hear what the man was saying and to whom.

He used the sturdy branches and made like a monkey, swinging overhead and keeping his movements smooth and silent, but snow rustled and fell to the ground. Thankfully, it mixed with the already falling snow and the abductor would be none the wiser.

As he neared, Bridge low-whistled and waited. At first it didn't seem like Wendy noticed and he started to whistle again, but she glanced upward as soon as the masked man turned his attention away. She shook her head, signaling him to wait, but wiggled her free hands. The woman was resourceful and quick.

Finally Bridge was close enough to hear the man's baritone voice. "I understand. Bear Valley. I'll call you when I'm twenty minutes out. No funny business." He ended the call, and knelt in front of Wendy. "Once we arrive in Bear Valley at the Rustic Resorts & Lodge, the money is mine," the man said. "I don't know what makes you so valuable and I don't care. But one thing is certain. You best not make trouble or I'll have to hurt you again, and maybe even negotiate that figure. What do you think?"

"I think you underestimate the fact I'm a woman. I *let* you punch me. I *allowed* you to take me. I practically stood with my arms up. Because now I know the drop point." Wendy's words cued Bridge she was ready for him to make a move.

Snowflakes fell heavier and thicker, and without movement to warm her up, Molly would be too cold inside that log. Time was short.

"What are you talking about?" the man asked.

"I'm talking about this," Wendy said and headbutted him so hard Bridge could almost feel it. The man fell backward and Wendy sprang on him. Bridge jumped from the tree as the man and Wendy rolled in the snow. As the man reared back his fist, Bridge caught it, startling him and giving Wendy a chance to spring to her feet. Bridge punched the attacker and he returned the jab, knocking him back. Wendy tackled him and a fight ensued. The attacker clocked her and stars spun inside her head, giving him just enough time to jump up and bolt into the woods.

They could chase him down but they'd already received the information they needed. If he returned, they'd deal with him. Wendy wasn't excited over taking lives. But it was a part of her job; the part that stuck to you like a bad meal always threatening to come back up. Stealing your sleep and thoughts. But it was kill or be killed. This wasn't a fairy tale where no one had to die. This was a dark reality that while people slept safe in their beds, people like him and Wendy were making it so those same people could sleep safe at night.

"You okay?" Bridge asked.

"No. But we do have a rendezvous point and you're safe. Also we have more weapons and ammo."

"We need to use that satellite phone right now and call my team in to rescue us and to fill them in on the drop site. We can rally a plan then."

"Where's Molly?" she asked, surveying the perimeter and ignoring his comments about calling his team. "I feel like a million people are on this mountain after me." She scanned the woods again. "Where's Molly?" Her voice was raised with concern.

"Safe. In a log about a quarter mile back. Let's go," Bridge clipped, unable to suppress his irritation now that Wendy was safe. He began the backward trek. "We need to use that phone."

"No."

Bridge paused, stunned. "What do you mean no?"

"I trust no one. Not even your team. I will protect Molly. I will make sure we descend this mountain and I will make it to that rendezvous point and take down Anderson Crawley, reclaim my life and reputation and deliver Molly to her uncle."

Bridge's hackles raised and his blood raced hot at her words. "I hear a lot of *I* in those statements but I'm here and saving your bacon and it's my job to protect Molly too. It's as if you don't think I'm able or you see me as a third wheel. What is wrong with you?"

"You're *mad* at me?" Wendy asked as if she couldn't fathom why he would be. "Why would you be mad at me? I've done nothing but protect you and Molly. I have a black eye and bruised ribs to prove it." Wendy's cheeks reddened and a vein bulged in her neck. Now she was as fired up as Bridge.

"Why am I mad at you? Let's see," he said with a monster dose of sarcasm. "For going rogue and being captured and not clueing me in that you might take the opportunity to allow yourself to be captured? Or for letting that guy hit you like that? For leaving me the first time? Cutting me twice? Arguing with me? Scaring me half to death? Forcing me to leave a child we both care deeply about alone in the woods with assassins and bears and other animals? There's so many reasons. Pick one. Spin the wheel or roll the dice."

Wendy released a heavy breath. "So I deserve all of that, but we have to separate personal from professional. Professionally, I am doing what I know to be right and good for everyone I'm entrusted with. And you're not making any calls. You have to understand—"

Bridge spun on her. "I don't have to understand anything! I've wondered for over three years if you were dead or alive, and I finally get you back and you go and do the same stupid thing you did before, only this time I could track you. Find you. You scared me! Don't you even care? Are you that compartmentalized or heartless? I loved you, Wendy. And I—I don't know how I feel now, but I know it's not hate or hoping you'd die. We are in this together, but you don't know *together* to save your life. You've always been on your own and I realize that—it's the job. And you didn't have family but I was going to be your family and all you've done is prove you don't want a partner. You want to be alone. Just you against the world." He waved his hand. This entire diatribe was pointless and falling on deaf ears but then he spoke again, still fired up.

"You never trusted me and that's become crystal clear. It's best we didn't end up married because marriages don't work if the couple can't trust one another."

"I do trust you, Bridge! I've left you alone with Molly haven't I? I didn't tie you to a tree, did I?"

If he were a dragon, he'd be breathing fire this very second. He thrust his finger in her face. "I dare you to try it. See what happens."

"And I dare you to take this phone. I am alone, Bridge. You have a top phantom in your unit. Connect the dots," she hissed.

Top Phantom...that could only mean one thing. "Archer? Archer Crow's a phantom?"

"Archer Crow is a lot of things. Now keep walking and stop talking!"

Bridge worked for Spears & Bow. He'd known former FBI agent Axel Spears for a couple of decades. Archer, Axel's business partner, was a bit murkier. The team knew their cofounder and boss had been a CIA operative, but the rest was murky. Archer worked behind the scenes and on Zoom calls, always had a fake background as if he didn't want them to know his location.

Bridge had always assumed it was old habits dying hard from being a CIA agent. That the man was overly cautious and extremely private, but those quirks had never raised suspicion about him as a person. Axel trusted him. Bridge and the rest of the bodyguard team did too.

Wendy didn't trust Archer Crow? What did she know that Bridge might not? "First of all, don't tell me what to do. You aren't my mama. Secondly, if you trusted me, you'd give me that phone. My team is solid. And if it's not, then I want concrete proof that Archer is some kind of leak."

"Bridge—"

He held up his hand. "Do you hear that?"

She paused, then her eyes widened. "ATVs."

"More than one. Move. We have to get Molly. Now!" Bridge bolted into action, Wendy right behind him.

Gunfire erupted and Wendy shrieked.

She'd been hit. In the shoulder and she wasn't sure how bad. There was no time to stop and look now. "We can't lead them back to her, Bridge. Molly's safer in a log than anywhere near us. Let's lose them, then circle back."

"What if they've found her? Used her to get to us? That's one thing that would make me drop my weapon, Wendy. Her safety."

Not Wendy's. He'd just lit her up all kinds of good and she had deserved the verbal lashing—personally. Professionally this was her life and she had to go with her gut. Maybe he should trust her! Except her track record was marred in his eyes. Why couldn't he see she had been safeguarding him and his family, and she was trying to do that now with Molly?

What if Archer Crow was on the inside? Molly would be delivered up to him and to Anderson. Until she had proof that Molly was safe with Spears & Bow, Bridge could kiss a phone call to his team goodbye, even if it meant running in these mountains for a few more days. Molly would be protected. She would make sure of it.

It was only a matter of time before Anderson realized Molly was the missing piece of code. He couldn't come within miles of her. She was safer out here with Wendy, and that's with all the peril.

Bridge's sharp intake of breath yanked her attention. "You're hit, Wendy. How bad?" His nostrils flared above that set jaw.

"Not sure and no time to worry about it now." Even if it did feel like fire. Another bullet hit a tree two feet in front of her and she skidded to a halt, ducking behind a pine and pulling the sniper rifle. "Open my backpack." She slung it to him. "Grenades are in there. Dude brought grenades. Don't ask me why."

She raised the scope to her eye, training her sights on the rise, waiting for the ATV to come up over the hill. "Just a second more..." A red

ATV broke through the tree line and Wendy pulled the trigger. The driver fell backward from the ATV and the vehicle ran into a tree, raining down snow from the branches and bark.

Bridge sprinted and jumped on the ATV, reversing it and then moving forward. "Still works!"

Another ATV gave chase and he pulled the pin on the grenade and tossed it toward the other while gunning it. As Bridge approached Wendy, she jumped on and he kept going.

The flash-bang blew snow and debris so high it provided a covering, and then the explosion echoed and fire caught. The last thing she wanted was a forest fire but with all the rain and snow it wouldn't spread. Unless there was another ATV out there, they were safe for now.

But it wouldn't last long. The all-terrain vehicles might be gone but the people hunting her were not. It was like they'd stepped on an ant hill and the swarms were out. Her heart raced inside her chest, beating wildly against her ribs but the vehicle would give them so much more speed down the mountain.

Bridge brought them to the hollowed-out log and Wendy jumped off, racing to it and to Molly. When she spotted the little girl inside with her fidget spinner, she nearly sobbed with relief.

She'd feared someone might have kidnapped her to use as leverage or ransom.

"Hi, Nanny Wendy," Molly said with such calm and ease and even joy—as joyous as Molly became. It was hard to detect unless a person knew her and Wendy had spent a lot of time with her as her nanny. "I knew Bridge would find you. He's a hero."

Did little Molly Wingbender have a little crush on Bridge? Wendy turned to see him on the ATV, his backpack on and a beard growing fuller, and felt her own stomach flutter. Did she have a crush on him too? Not at the moment. He was being unreasonable and refusing to see her side of things. He'd handed her backside to her all the way here.

He'd harbored so many ill feelings toward her but he also made valid points. She was rogue. A loner her whole life. As an only child and then as an orphan. Just her against the world. When she went into the CIA and Anderson trained her, it had been for solo missions, except the time she'd worked with Archer Crow—the phantom.

Bridge's words still stung like a hive of bees. He'd touched a nerve that revealed the truth. She'd been so used to depending on herself she found it challenging to trust and depend on others and even on God at times. She'd always tried to figure her own way out of things. But in the

North Korean prison, she'd learned all she had was God. So why couldn't she trust Bridge now and rely on him? Wendy should have told him her plans. That if he awoke and she was gone, he'd know why. That he could track her prints in the snow but not to worry because if he didn't find her, she'd find him once she'd learned the rendezvous point she was to be taken to. Sure, right now Anderson had no idea she'd broken free of the attacker and knew the drop-off location. She had an advantage now. He'd never see her coming until she wanted him to.

But in the process she'd once again broken trust with Bridge. Went off on her own and forced him into a dangerous situation. She didn't want there to be mistrust between the two of them. If she had to pick one person in the whole world to have her back, it would be Bridge Spencer. Hands down. After this stunt, she would bank on the fact Bridge would never choose her—to have his back in the field or be his partner in life. The thought ate a massive hole in her gut but even so, for now, he was not calling his team.

She helped Molly to her feet and dusted the snow and earthy debris from her backside. "You want to take a ride?" she asked.

"Yes. I want to go home and Bridge said I can

have a cheeseburger with bacon and no onions or tomato."

"You definitely can. That sounds amazing." They'd gone quite a long time since their meal of fish, and fish didn't stay on the stomach long. "For now, do you want peanut butter crackers or another granola bar?"

"Granola bar."

Wendy handed her a chocolate chip bar and led her to the ATV where Bridge waited with a sly grin. "Your chariot awaits, milady."

"This is not a chariot. A chariot is a two-wheeled horse-drawn vehicle used in ancient warfare and racing."

"Did you read that in the Oxford Languages online dictionary?" he asked and Wendy held in her laughter.

"I did."

"Yes, I thought you might have."

Molly paused before climbing on the ATV. "I think you might be joking. Are you joking?"

She had picked up on Bridge's nuances and figured out when he was teasing.

"I am. I know you have it memorized. Hop on behind me, and Nanny Wendy can sit behind you on the back."

Molly obeyed and climbed on, putting her arms around Bridge, and Wendy felt a tinge of jealousy. She climbed on behind Molly and held on to the metal rack. "Ready!" she called and Bridge hit the gas.

The wind was fierce but at least Molly was shielded between the two of them. Which was good as her nose was runny and red and her eyes appeared glassy. Wendy brought her hand around. "I want to check you for fever."

When Molly nodded, she touched her forehead. Slightly warm but not terrible. Maybe low-grade fever. They needed to get this child to a warm place with water and food. She might be dehydrated. Once they stopped, she'd see to it she had some hydration. But she wanted a cheeseburger and a granola bar. She might not be too sick since she hadn't lost her appetite. Wendy would take the small blessing.

They were to meet in Bear Valley at the Rustic Resorts & Lodge. It was nestled in the mountains, popular so there would be people around but remote enough she could be extracted without anyone noticing. Was it coincidence Anderson had chosen Bear Valley since one of Wendy's safe houses was here? How would he have known that? No one knew.

Wendy, like any good spy, kept several safe havens that no one else on the planet would ever know about. She had one in Madrid, one in the countryside in Scotland and one in Bear Valley. How would Anderson know or was it just close to the horse camp where Molly had been bait to attract Wendy? Only Anderson would have known that—but how did he know Molly was at this horse camp? And what were the odds that Bridge would be her guardian?

Once they found a safe place, she was going to call David Wingbender and find out who he might have told or if anything had been off lately with people around. Also Bridge had asked a question earlier that she'd originally let go but now wondered about.

Molly's mom.

Had she died or vanished? She would have known about Charlie's work since the Mask project had been his for decades. If she'd died, then why was there confusion about her?

If she was alive, could she be connected to Anderson? Someone had to know Molly's location in order to tip off Wendy about an abduction attempt again, thereby drawing Wendy out. There had already been that one botched attempt that led to David sending Molly here for protection in the first place. Why did David choose Bridge's company? Who referred them to David? That person might be behind this, working for Anderson. David would not have known about Bridge's connection to Wendy, and he'd have had no way to know that Bridge would even be assigned to this mission.

Why had Axel Spears chosen Bridge? Maybe he hadn't. It was possible Archer Crow requested him through Axel. A lot of chance was going on here or else Wendy simply didn't see the full picture. But she planned to find out.

Wendy had already planned to find Molly and hide her away. She was in danger as the last missing piece of code. But the tip Talia received and passed on came from an anonymous source that couldn't be traced. Wendy had known danger would be close, which was why she'd packed a survival kit.

Bridge suspected Talia, but not Wendy. Talia had proven nothing but trustworthy. Wendy had warned her to regularly sweep for bugs in her office, home, laptop and phones, though as a tech specialist she already practiced this. Anderson knew they were close and likely suspected at some point Wendy might reach out to Talia for help or information and that Talia might give it freely.

Wendy hadn't mentioned sweeping Talia's car and Talia might not have thought of it either. Someone might have bugged her vehicle. Wendy trusted no one other than Talia and Bridge, but it didn't appear that way. She had to make him believe he had her trust and loyalty.

She had no idea how to accomplish that though. For now she had to focus on descending this mountain and making sure Molly was safe and received medical attention. Wendy could use a doctor herself. The gunshot wound burned like wildfire, but the fact it hadn't knocked her out or bled any worse told her it was probably a flesh wound that might need a few stitches, if that.

How much farther did they have to go? The sound of their ATV could call attention to them, but they needed the speed, to eat up the ground and get them off the mountain faster. Once they reached the bottom, Bear Valley was about thirty minutes away. They'd need a car or Uber or something.

"I don't think we're too far from a mountain road now," Bridge hollered.

"Good. We might be out of the danger zone."

As soon as she voiced that hope, a bullet hit the side of the ATV. Molly shrieked and Bridge made a hard right. The two left wheels came off the ground.

"We're going to crash!" Wendy yelled and held Molly with all her might.

ELEVEN

Bridge used all his strength to readjust the handles on the ATV and bring them upright, but the gunfire continued. Wendy fired off a few rounds in the direction the bullets were flying but whoever was shooting also had an ATV and it was roaring right toward them.

"I'm scared!" Molly cried.

"I know, baby. Hang on to me," Bridge said. If a bullet hit the gas tank, they'd all be toast. But they needed this vehicle to get down to the mountain road. They were so close.

Another shot hit and blew out the tire and the ATV jerked. Bridge was losing steering power. He tapped the brakes to slow them down but they were sluggish to respond. "You need to jump with her. We're gonna hit a tree. I can't control the speed. Jump, Wendy! Now!"

Wendy snatched Molly, hurling her off the ATV, and Bridge watched in horror as Wendy rotated midair so she would take the brunt of the impact. She landed on her back, her head hitting a tree. Bridge tried to slow the ATV but something must have been hit. The brakes weren't working. He jumped too and hit the ground, rolling to a stop, his breath knocked out of his lungs. He heard the other ATV heading right for them.

Wendy was already up, but her cheeks were pale and blood dripped down her face from where she'd hit her head. Molly stood beside her, shaking and wide-eyed. He was pretty sure she was going into shock and was somewhat surprised the child hadn't already experienced it, given all they'd been through. He and Wendy were trained for this, and it was overwhelming. He couldn't imagine a civilian, let alone a child, not being traumatized.

As the ATV approached, Bridge followed Wendy and Molly into the thicket. Another bullet was fired, only this time the driver of the ATV fell off his vehicle as it ran into a tree, crunching and dying.

Wendy came out of the thicket she and Molly had dove into, her rifle in hand. "I got him." Then she fell to the ground in a crumpled heap.

"Wendy!" Bridge raced to her and checked her pulse, thankful she had one. Wendy had only passed out, probably from a concussion when her head hit the tree. Blood trickled from the wound, but didn't need stitches. She did need ice though as a goose egg swelled. Now to check the bullet wound to her shoulder. She was like a human pincushion, and he ached at her pain.

The bullet wound did need stitches unfortunately. Next he checked on Molly. Her pupils were too large. Her pulse too fast.

They did not have time to stick around, but they both needed serious medical attention. Bridge pulled out the rolled-up sleeping bag and yanked it from the case and draped it over Molly, then forced her to drink a whole bottle of water for hydration. Once he'd seen to her, Wendy roused.

"I hit my head," she said, reaching up a hand to touch it.

"You did and then you passed out. Molly's in mild shock but I have a blanket on her and gave her water." He handed her a bottle. "Drink."

She didn't argue and sucked down the entire bottle.

"You need stitches to your shoulder and I have a needle and sutures. You up for it?"

Wendy groaned but nodded. "Do what you have to do but not in front of Molly."

Like he'd been born yesterday. He bit down on the sarcasm and grabbed the first-aid kit, then moved her behind a tree but where he could still keep an eye on Molly. First he poured rubbing alcohol on his hands and then to her wound, which sent her off the ground but she didn't cry out.

"Sorry," he said. "This is going to hurt."

"Just get it done," she said through gritted teeth.

Bridge ran the sutures through the eye of the needle. "Take a deep breath."

She did, and on the inhale, he inserted the needle into her flesh. She ground her teeth but kept quiet as he sewed three stitches and tied it off. Then he gave her three pain relievers from the kit and another bottle of water. "Trust me, you'll want these."

Wendy downed them, then rose to her feet. "We need to get out of here."

"Who you tellin'?" he said and then they checked Molly again. "Molly, can you walk with us out of here?" She didn't respond. "Molly, I know this is hard and scary but we're almost to a town and that means getting you warm, dry and safe."

She looked up at him. "I can walk."

Good. Relief eased his tight muscles. "Then let's go."

Bridge noticed Wendy moving at a slower pace and it wasn't to keep up with Molly. She was hurt. Exhausted and probably even nauseous from the head wound. But she was brave and a total trooper and she forged ahead until they finally broke out onto a mountain road. "The town is just below," he told her.

A red pickup truck neared them and Wendy put her hand on her weapon and Bridge did the same. The truck slowed and he saw an older man with a long gray beard behind the wheel. But Bridge trusted no one. Especially if Anderson Crawley was using phantoms.

"Woohee, y'all be looking like hammered toast. Can I help ya?" the mountain man asked.

Bridge looked to Wendy who was studying the gentleman with wary eyes. Anyone could be a killer in disguise. They were paranoid but with every right to be at this point.

"Look, I don't often pick up strangers. Not in this day and age but your little girl looks sick and, ma'am, no offense but you're looking worse for wear too." He eyed Bridge as if he'd been the one to black her eye. "Good Lord would expect me to do the neighborly thing and that would be to help you get somewhere safe."

Wendy looked at Bridge again and nodded. They were both packing, and if things went sideways, between the two of them they'd have it covered. But deep within Bridge felt like this man was a true godsend. God knew they needed help and Wendy and Molly might not make the walk into town. The sign on the road said ten miles.

Bridge climbed in the truck first, then Wendy and Molly.

"Where can I drop you folks?" the driver asked and Bridge noticed Southern Gospel playing on the radio. Reminded him of the music his own father had often played on Sunday mornings while they were getting ready for church.

Wendy rattled off her address for her safe house. A place even Bridge had never known about. How much more had Wendy kept from him, not trusted him with?

"Oh, nice area. Lot of land over there. I worry it'll sell to commercial folks. They're building up every square inch here for tourism, but we won't have any beautiful land to enjoy if they keep doing that." He continued to make small talk as he drove into the heart of Bear Valley, a picturesque southern mountain town with bear statues outside most businesses. People were out in this weather shopping. No wonder Wendy had a safe house here. It was a beautiful place. "You should see a doctor, ma'am. That eye is pretty swollen."

"I'm fine. Really."

The man shrugged and simply went on talking about the town and the changes and maybe the Lord would come before all the wildlife went extinct from cutting down their habitat. Bridge was thankful for the distraction as he watched behind them and all around. This wasn't over yet.

Once at Wendy's safe house, they'd have to

make a game plan. One where they went up against the formidable CIA and won.

Bridge didn't think the scenario was going to come without casualties.

Wendy thanked the man for his help and God for bringing them someone safe to help them when they needed it most. She could have pushed through even feeling as weak, tired and sore as she was. She'd been trained to push through exhaustion, hunger and pain. But not little Molly. Her cheeks were flushed and her eyes glassy. She would never have made a ten-mile walk into town and then from there to the little cabin Wendy had purchased in cash years ago.

It was a quaint two-bedroom with sparse amenities, but everything she would need if she had to lay low for a period of time. Nothing but woods surrounded the house. She'd loved it for the scenery and the privacy. After the mountain man drove away, they padded up the porch steps and Wendy entered a code. The front door unlocked and they went inside.

"Molly, how about I take you into the guest bathroom and set up a hot shower for you and then I'll make us something to eat." Molly was about five feet and Wendy had several inches on her but she would probably fit into some of her leggings and a sweatshirt. The child needed something warm and comfortable to wear. In the meantime she could wash her clothing. They all stunk to high heaven.

"Okay."

"Let me take that necklace so it doesn't get wet." She unhooked the locket and pocketed it.

"Nanny Wendy?"

"Yes?"

"Are we safe?"

"Yes. We are now." That much she at least hoped to be true. She and Bridge were careful, but they couldn't be sure no one had seen them as they reached the road and climbed into the vehicle, then rode to the safe house. But she had security cameras set up and an app on her phone that gave her 24/7 access to the perimeter. "Get all warm and toasty in the water and I'll give you something to wear." She left her in the bathroom and headed into the living room where Bridge sat with his head leaning on the back of the sofa.

"How is she?" he asked without opening his eyes.

"Sick. I'm going to grab her some clothing and medicine. Best thing she can do right now is eat and sleep." She wished she could do the same. "We have about an hour until we're supposed to be at the lodge for the swap."

"Wendy, you need to let me call my team. A

child is missing and I'm sure David Wingbender has been on their behinds every five seconds to find his niece. Do you think I'd join a team that might be crooked?"

Wendy grit her teeth. They'd been at this before. Archer Crow could be the phantom. He would have ways others wouldn't to find them. But as she looked at Bridge, she realized this decision might be a step in the right direction for them both. She needed to let go of control and stop believing there was no one else to help her. This would go a long way with Bridge. He deserved her complete trust. And she did need help. Wendy couldn't fight this battle alone and battles were never supposed to be fought alone. She thought of Moses and his friends holding his hands up when he was too exhausted to keep them up himself. But they had to stay raised to gain victory. Victory, she realized now, came with help. Help from friends, allies and God.

"No. I don't think that," she told him. "Call them. Tell them where we are and that we have Molly and she's safe. Tell them everything. I need help, Bridge, and you're the one person I do trust. Though I haven't shown it. Ever. It's been hard for me to not go it alone. It's my default setting."

Bridge stared at her, his mouth hanging open. "You mean it?"

"I do. I have reservations. Not gonna lie. But I trust you." She frowned.

"What is it?"

"It's just some things are bothering me. I know we were—are—being hunted but that's a big mountain. Someone always knew where we were and, yes, the footprints in the snow weren't working on our behalf but it seems to me these hunters knew exactly where we were. Don't you find that odd?"

"Yeah but no one on my team would GPS track me and give information to Anderson."

"Me neither. I mean I'm not bugged." She grabbed her backpack and pulled out her cell phone. She hadn't been able to use it and it still had battery life. But she had extra chargers and cords in the kitchen drawer. "I need to call Talia."

"I don't want you to do that, Wendy. I know you're giving me a long leash of trust here, and I appreciate it but CIA spies are known for being double agents and I would prefer to go through Spears & Bow alone. Would you trust me on this too?"

Wendy trusted Talia. She wasn't a part of this with Anderson. But Bridge was asking this of her and she wanted to give him his request because last time she hadn't. In all that had happened, one thing she knew. She still loved Bridge

Spencer. Once it had been with most of her heart and now she wanted to show him he had all of her heart. Fully. Completely. Whether or not he wanted her remained to be seen and now wasn't the time to ask. Wendy needed to prove through her actions she meant what she said.

"Okay. I won't call her or anyone you don't want me to and we'll figure out the game plan together. No going rogue, Bridge." She held back tears because what would she do if Bridge didn't want her? If he was too hurt to give her a second chance? Her world would crumble. Could she live without Bridge? Yes. God would give her strength and be her source of comfort. Did she want to live a life without him? No. Not in the least.

Bridge sat forward, looking her dead in the eyes. His soft, sweet amber eyes drew her in. "This means a lot to me, Wendy. I'm not taking it or your safety lightly."

"I know," she murmured. "So what's the plan?" *Release the reins*, she told herself. *Be a real partner. A follower as well as a leader.*

"I could go with a mask on. Pretend to be your captor. With all your injuries, it's believable. What do you think?" he asked.

He was bringing her in as an equal. This was what partnership was. "Anderson is one of the most brilliant tactical minds I know. He was former military before CIA. He won't allow you to stay in a mask. He'll want to see your face. He might be in a mask, but you can't be."

Bridge inhaled deeply. "I thought that might be the case. I'm going to call the team. I know they're nearby."

"Nanny Wendy. I need you," Molly called.

"Do what you need to," Wendy told him. "Give them the address, but one of them needs to stay here and protect Molly. She can't go and she's sick." She darted off, grabbed clothing for Molly and slid it through the cracked door.

"Do you feel better?" she asked Molly.

"A little."

After Molly exited the bathroom, Wendy gave her some Tylenol and cold-and-flu medicine. "You hungry?"

She nodded.

"Why don't you lie on the couch and Bridge can turn on some TV for you if you'd like that and I'll fix us some soup." Wendy had kept a few streaming services and took care of the utilities even though she wasn't often here—only to drop most of the flash drives into her safe. The others were in her safe in Florida. Groceries were a different story. All she had on hand was frozen and canned foods. She didn't often come and hadn't stocked the fridge in ages.

Molly crawled onto the couch and Bridge covered her up and handed her the remote. She went straight to YouTube and began watching a gamer play *Minecraft*. Bridge left the room for privacy and called Axel Spears while Wendy opened up several cans of chicken noodle soup, then found a new box of crackers. She put the electric kettle on for hot tea and then Bridge returned.

"They've been worried sick. David too. They told him not to come in from LA until they had Molly so they're going to call him and he can fly in later tonight. I told him to bring cosmetics in case Anderson has facial recognition devices under his belt. I'm in the system as former FBI. Contacts, full beard and mustache and a modulator chip attached to my throat will bypass it. Since it's not a handheld, Anderson won't see it. And if he's using voice recognition software it won't pick up the modulator chip. Helps having a spy on the team." Bridge smirked.

She hoped he was right. "Good. When will they arrive?"

"Be here in twenty. They've been canvassing the surrounding towns around the horse camp and flying drones over the mountain but the snow and rain haven't made it easy."

Wendy dished out bowls of soup and put one on a tray with crackers, hot tea, water, a spoon and a napkin. She carried it to Molly, who scooted up, and Wendy propped a pillow behind her, then set the tray over her lap. "There's plenty, so if you want more, you can have all you like. We don't have to ration anymore. I also found some of those cream-filled snack cakes you like and I'll bring you one of those after you eat the soup."

"Thank you, Nanny Wendy. Chicken noodle soup is my favorite."

"I know." She knelt. "Can I hug you, Molly?"

Molly paused, then nodded, and Wendy lightly hugged her but she wanted to hold on tightly and never let go. She did though and Molly smiled. It was nice to see she'd enjoyed the physical contact—or at least welcomed it. She returned to the kitchen and sat across from Bridge, eating their meal in silence. They were ravenous, eating two and three portions. Molly devoured half a sleeve of saltines before the doorbell rang.

"They're here," Bridge said.

Wendy peered out the window. Three out of four were here. Where was Archer Crow aka Phantom?

TWELVE

Bridge opened the door and Axel, his boss, loomed on the front porch looking like a regular bigfoot out there. Behind him were Libby Winters and Amber Rathbone. Both women were southern state natives like Axel from Texas. Only Archer was from the Midwest but he wasn't here. Bridge wasn't surprised. The man worked more behind the scenes, though Bridge wasn't sure why. Archer was a mystery but he wasn't going to voice that to Wendy. She already had suspicious vibes over him. However she had chosen to trust Bridge and humbled herself. Bridge had been stunned and waited for the punch line but one hadn't come.

Maybe Wendy had finally realized she didn't have to shoulder everything alone, and could trust Bridge to help and not hinder. The whole world *wasn't* on her shoulders. They were on God's. If Wendy showed him trust in this way, what was she truly trying to reveal? Was it an olive branch to say she understood what partnership meant and she saw him as one? Or might there be something stronger and deeper—on an emotional level? If that were the case, could Bridge trust her with his heart again?

That was a tough question that would take a lot of prayerful consideration. But one he wanted to contemplate and pray about. Wendy had never been away from his heart, just shoved down deep and closed off. But always hovering behind the locked door.

The team stepped inside and Bridge introduced them to Wendy.

Libby had her dark hair in its signature ponytail, her sharp blue eyes always on alert, observing. A former Secret Service agent, she was tough, intelligent and perceptive. Amber had softer features and intense dark eyes. Amber was astute but less reserved than Libby, even if she kept her personal life as locked up as the rest of them.

"You look like you battled a tornado," Libby said to Wendy.

"I feel like I have. Thanks for coming. Are you hungry? We have soup and crackers."

Libby smiled. "We're good. Thanks."

Amber had already spotted Molly on the couch. "Hey, sweetie."

"I'm not sweetie. I'm Molly."

Amber's eye widened and she nodded. "Good to know." She glanced at Wendy. Wendy mouthed, "She's literal about everything."

Nodding, Amber grinned. "Well, it's nice to meet you, Molly."

Molly didn't answer. She kept her eyes glued on the YouTube channel.

Amber shoved her hands in her pocket. "What's our plan?"

Bridge laid out the idea. "We good?"

Libby and Axel looked at one another, speaking with their eyes. The way he and Wendy could carry on conversations they didn't want others privy to. What was going on?

"I like the idea of the makeup and we brought the disguise kit," Libby said. "However, it's best if Axel goes with Wendy and not you, Bridge."

"Why?" Bridge wanted to be with her every step of the way. Not that he didn't trust his team, but this was…this was Wendy. He needed to see it through by her side. He glanced at Wendy, her mouth grim, but she didn't protest.

Libby cleared her throat, looked at Axel as if for him to continue, but when he simply stared at her, she frowned. "You're too close to this, Bridge. And when you care deeply for someone, you make mistakes." She rubbed the scar running across her throat. "You don't take care of yourself when you should and it could turn rough in there. We don't think you will do what's necessary if it comes down to the wire. And Axel will."

"What do you mean?"

"It's okay." Wendy nodded. "Axel, I trust you. Bridge, you can be nearby. Backup. Molly needs someone if it goes sideways and it could."

"I don't like it. I don't understand." He could feel his hackles start to rise. "But if you'd rather have Axel by your side, then fine."

Wendy pinched the bridge of her nose. "It's not like that."

Finally it sunk into Bridge's thick skull. Wendy's eye was swollen and black from one of her captors. Could Bridge purposely hurt her if it came to that in front of Anderson? No. Libby was right; he couldn't be objective when it came to Wendy. He couldn't physically harm her for the sake of keeping up the ruse, nor could he watch her be harmed.

But Axel could. He'd hate every second and never let it go too far, but he could do what Bridge could not. "You're right. Okay."

Libby turned to Axel. "You ready then?"

Axel smirked. "Definitely." He held up a black toiletry bag. "Gonna go work on my makeup."

Libby snorted. "I'll help."

"What? You don't think I can disguise myself good enough?"

"No. Not really." She followed him to the bathroom and Amber sat at the table. "I'll stay with Molly and we'll become fast friends."

"She's sick," Wendy said. "I gave her cold meds about forty minutes ago and Tylenol. Keep fluids down her."

Amber grinned. "You love her, don't you?"

"I'm pretty attached, yes. I trust you to take care of her though. And trust isn't easy for me. But if Bridge trusts you, then I will too."

"I appreciate that. I never had kids of my own but I've always wanted them. I'll keep her safe no matter what happens. You have my word."

Bridge watched as the two formed a friendship over the safety of this precious little girl they'd all fallen in love with. Later, when they were about to leave, he sat beside Molly. "Molly, I won't lie it's going to be dangerous but we will return. Remember when we talked about hope in Jesus being foolproof?"

"Yes, I told you I wouldn't forget and I'd remind you if you forgot. But you didn't."

Bridge grinned. "No, I didn't. Hope in Jesus means trusting Him in all situations no matter what. Even though we can't see Jesus, we trust and believe He is with us. That He's real. Has anyone talked to you about Jesus before?"

"Nanny Wendy. I do believe in Jesus, Bridge. That's why I know we will be safe."

"Right. You hope in Him and He will work all things out for our good, even if it feels like we're in a bad situation."

"Oh. Okay."

Wendy had not only protected her but she'd led her to Jesus. He loved this kid. He didn't want to think about his feelings for Wendy.

Axel returned with a fuller beard than he'd had before, along with a mustache and green contacts and he'd used some latex to make his nose a little hawkish. Bridge wouldn't have known him if not for the massive build and slight swagger in his gait. "Wendy, do you have the flash drives of all the codes?"

"Most of them are here in a secure safe but the others are in Florida. Both safes are hidden and virtually impossible to break into."

"Good. I want to put a microphone on you but Anderson Crawley will run a bug sweep over you as well as a pat down. I have a high-tech mic that would work but I have to inject it under your skin. It'll pick up like a dream but won't be detected by a bug sweeper because the skin protects it. It'll sting, but looking at your face, I'm thinking you can handle a sting."

Wendy laughed. "Can't be any worse than Bridge dumping a bottle of rubbing alcohol over a gunshot wound and stitching me up with no lidocaine."

"You're tough. I like it. I can remove the chip as easy as I can inject it. Small incision."

"I'm down." Wendy said.

Axel retrieved what looked like a glue gun. "I'm going to insert it near the collar bone so it'll pick up better than in your arm."

Wendy pulled the neck of her shirt down and Axel swabbed the area with an alcohol wipe, then he raised the gun. "Inhale and hold it, please."

She did.

Axel shot the little microphone chip into her skin. Wendy didn't even wince.

"Check, check," he said.

"I hear you loud and clear," Libby called from the bathroom. She returned with his toiletry bag. "We'll be able to hear you from a quarter of a mile away with that, Wendy. We need you to persuade Anderson Crawley to admit to applying a deepfake to the video footage of Charlie's death. But even if he doesn't admit it, with the pieces of code in place, we can prove it was doctored and that will help clear your name. I assume you copied the footage before running."

Wendy nodded. "I want Anderson. He needs to be brought to justice for treason on top of a million other charges." Her jaw hardened and Libby agreed.

"One thing at a time. Does everyone know their parts?" Libby asked.

Wendy approached Molly and rubbed at her collarbone where the mic had been injected. "Miss Amber is going to stay with you for a while. You can trust her and she will keep you safe. We have some work to do and then we'll be back for you. Is that okay?"

"I trust you and Bridge, Nanny Wendy."

"Maybe you can recite the dogs in alphabetical order for Miss Amber. She'll love that." Bridge winked at Wendy and she laughed.

"I do love dogs," Amber said. "I had a German shepherd named Sheila when I was a K-9 patrol officer in Memphis before becoming a detective."

"I want a Shetland sheepdog," Molly said. "But you can't have them at boarding school. And I go to boarding school. Did you go to boarding school?" Molly asked.

"No, I went to public school, but my dad was allergic to dogs so we never had one growing up. I always wanted one though." Amber smiled at Wendy and Bridge. "We'll be perfectly fine. No worries."

"Let's do this." Axel grabbed his gear. "Y'all don't mind if I pray over us first, do you?"

No one had any qualms about a prayer and Axel led them in one for wisdom, direction and protection and Molly's healing, then he stepped outside and called the number on the satellite phone and arranged the drop point as well as the proof-of-life video with today's date from an online paper.

When Bridge returned he laced his hand in Wendy's. "This will work." Before the team had arrived, Wendy had finally opened up and been transparent with her thoughts and why she had her reservations about Archer. And they'd formed their own game plan they'd pitched to the team.

Axel trusted Bridge and never questioned anything, however Bridge had left out the part where Wendy wasn't fully convinced Archer wasn't involved. But she was willing to give him—and ultimately Bridge—the benefit of the doubt.

"We know what and who we're up against. Time to flip the script," Libby said with a smirk, and Axel nodded. Bridge caught the admiration and something else glittering in Axel's eyes. A glitter he'd noticed often, actually, when it came to Libby Winters.

Amber sat beside Molly. "And we know exactly what to do here. You can trust I'll take excellent care of Molly. If you're worried about her, you'll make mistakes. We have no room for error if we want this to go off without a hitch."

"My throat hurts, Nanny Wendy," Molly said.

"Miss Amber is going to take you to the doctor in just a little while. You'll be right as rain."

"How is rain right?" she asked and Bridge grunted to mask his laugh. Wendy had walked into that one.

"It's a saying and, to be honest, I'm not sure what it means. You'll be cared for and safe with Miss Amber."

"I want my necklace back my mom gave me."

Bridge knelt in front of Molly. "We'll make sure you have it back. We need it for just a little bit, and then it's yours again."

She nodded, but she wasn't happy. Not having that locket was saving her life. But the less she knew, the better.

Bridge noticed the concern for Molly radiating in Wendy's eyes. He laced his fingers with hers and leaned in and whispered, "She's going to be in good hands."

She squeezed his fingers. "I know."

But they didn't truly know. They hoped.

They were going up against the best of the best and if they weren't on their A-game, this would go south fast.

Axel was to bring Wendy to cabin #10 on the edge of the resort, a private cabin nestled in the woods with a creek running behind. He'd bound Wendy's hands behind her back and secured her feet in shackles but he'd also given her a key, which Libby had secured behind the button of her jeans. If Anderson ran a scanning wand over her for weapons, it would beep but he'd assume it was the metal of her jeans button. However, she couldn't carry a weapon.

Her saving grace was she could free her hands from behind her back and use the key to unlock her feet; Wendy could fight with her feet as well if not better than her hands. She could also gain access to a gun or knife if needed. But it was dangerous and Bridge didn't love it. She'd seen that in his eyes but reassured him that she was going to be okay and his team would protect her. Libby and Bridge would be out of sight but nearby. They'd taken a vehicle Wendy kept as a backup in the garage. Anderson might have drones scanning for miles and could easily detect if anyone else was in the vehicle with her and her "captor." For this to go off properly, they had to think of everything.

Axel's phone rang and he hit the button on the phone that was attached to the dash. It filtered through the Bluetooth. "Well, well." Axel laughed. "You look nice."

"Woohee," the man said and Wendy snapped to attention. She knew that old hillbilly voice. "You en route?" the voice changed, gentle but deep. She looked at the FaceTime feed and saw it was the man from the truck. The one who'd picked them up and driven them to her safe house. But he'd lost his accent.

"We are." Axel glanced at Wendy and grinned. "Want to properly thank your road rescuer?"

She knew who the man was. Archer Crow. Still in his cosmetic disguise down to his age-stained teeth. The phantom. He'd been under their noses and neither of them—not even his own colleague—recognized him. Not even Wendy, who had worked a mission with him that had lasted over a month.

This was why he was the best of the best. Behind him was clouds. He was hiding his location and still keeping in costume. Why? Why not reveal his face?

"Archer?"

"Hi, Wendy. Sorry to hear about your predicament. If I'd have known, I would have tried to help you. But I've been out of the spy game and lost contact."

If he was out of the spy game, why keep so secretive and hide his face and background all the time?

"Were you burned too?" she asked him.

"No. I walked away and that's all you need to know. I wanted to be the one to pick you up. Show you that you have nothing to fear from me. I'm on your side and I can't be bought. And I wasn't lying. I felt God nudge me to be that person to rescue you and Bridge. It'll all work out. I trust my people and I know you're top notch. Saved my bacon in Russia. Twice."

She had. "When it's all over, Bridge and I owe you a dinner. It'll be good to catch up."

"Sorry, no can do. I have to get back. But when we heard Bridge had gone missing and Molly, I wanted to be there. Flew straight in and I'm leaving within the hour."

"Why can't you stay? Where are you going? Where's home?"

"You were always nosy. Comes with the job, I guess. My answer is the same for all three, old friend. None'ya."

Wendy chuckled. None of her business. Fair enough. "Well, take care, you old coot. You make for a believable mountain man."

"You should see me as a forty-year-old pregnant woman." He winked and Axel laughed.

Wendy shook her head. "I don't see that being very attractive."

"You'd be surprised." He waved and nodded to someone out of the screen. "Wheels up for me. Take care, Wendy. Later, Ax."

The call ended and Wendy stared at Axel.

"Archer knows you. He said the minute Bridge mentioned him—and he would at some point— you'd connect what seemed too coincidental to be true. And it was. We just got some of the details wrong at first. He said you'd never let Bridge contact us. And even if you did, you still wouldn't trust us even after. Spies have trust issues, he said. Imagine that."

Wendy snorted. "For real. He wanted us to know he rescued us. When he could have killed or taken Molly." And to be honest, Archer was so good that he might have been able to do it— to take Molly and put her and Bridge out permanently with his bare hands. Archer didn't look like muscle and brawn, though he was always fit. He was mild-mannered and looked more like a book nerd. That's what made him lethal. You never expected that kind of cunning and power until he'd already rendered a person useless or retrieved what he wanted. By the time the person realized they'd been duped, it was too late. He was in the wind.

Why would he have left the Agency? What had happened? She almost asked Axel but he'd give the same answer as Archer had. None'ya business.

Wendy was glad she ended up trusting Bridge. He'd been right all along.

And she'd also been right about that locket Molly wore. If she hadn't fidgeted with it, they might have never seen the truth.

Axel slowed as they wound through the mountain road to the cabin. Once they were there, he shifted in his seat. "I have to tell you something. Libby has the mic so Bridge can't hear. I need to make this look real. You understand that better than anyone and I didn't want to talk too much in depth while Bridge had ears, but I saw that you figured out why we wanted me to do this and not him. I know you two have a past and he cares about you. It's obvious he's protective."

"You want to manhandle me and maybe beat me up a little. Is that what you're saying?" Wendy smirked. She'd been through worse for the sake of a mission.

"Want to? Not even a little. But I might need to. And if he wants me to prove myself, he might ask me to do something that would hurt you, and I need you to know that I won't hesitate, but I won't find any joy in it either. I'm a good read of people, Wendy, and you're tough. Real tough. I know you can handle a punch or some roughing up but Bridge isn't gonna like that."

"No, he's not. Not that I'm looking forward to it but you do what you need to do and make it as real as you need to, without knocking me out. I need to be lucid. And I've already had a head injury so keep it to the core and kidneys maybe."

Axel laughed. "I like you. Kidney punches hurt."

"I'm acutely aware."

He pointed at her. "If things are chill with

you and Bridge when all this is over, I'm gonna offer you a job. Unless you plan to go back to Langley."

She hadn't thought about it too much. Her focus had been on finding the codes and clearing her name. At this point she had no idea what her future would hold.

Axel exited the vehicle and opened the passenger door, yanking Wendy out and not being gentle about it. He pushed her forward and she stumbled but righted herself as she worked to the rhythm of her foot shackles. She had to shuffle more than walk.

He gripped her by the back of her hair and forced her up the cabin steps onto the porch. A man in black including a full face mask with dark sunglasses came out with his gun aimed on them.

"Stop right there. Just need to do some scanning."

Another figure approached. Tall and slenderer, dressed the same. The figure wanded Wendy. Nothing beeped and he turned and nodded. All clear. No bugs. No mics and no weapons on Wendy.

"Your turn," the bigger one said. He was also using a modulator. He wouldn't risk Axel being able to identify the voice later on, like in a court hearing.

The slender figure—a runner, she'd guess—wanded Axel and it beeped. "You have a weapon."

"You're right I do and I'll be keeping it, thank you very much. At least until I have my money for this hag. What's some chick so valuable for?"

"You don't need to know that. I want the weapon or no deal."

"What's to say you won't shoot me as soon as I hand the little rabbit over?" Axel asked, his own voice modulated to sound rougher and grittier.

"Nothing. But if you want the money, you'll behave."

Axel relinquished the gun and knife and tossed them at the feet of the more sinewy man who collected them. "I want my money."

"Inside."

Axel pushed Wendy forward and into the cabin, the other man following. Inside a laptop sat on the table. The slender man sat. A man she knew well. "Account information."

Axel sat and rattled off the offshore account numbers and the man entered it into the system. In a few moments it showed the money had hit the account.

"I want to check that with my own bank."

"Of course."

Axel went into his phone and typed, then nodded. "Okay. Then I'm done here." He stood. "I'd watch her. She's sneaky and tough. Won't go lightly, as you can see." He pointed to Wendy's black and swollen eye.

The man laughed as he rose. "I'll be just fine."

Axel swaggered out of the cabin and he let him. He let him walk. Why would he do that? That wasn't like Anderson. Not at all. Wendy's stomach knotted, worried that the hammer was about to drop on an unsuspecting Axel Spears. A bomb in his car. A sniper in a tree. But the car started up and she heard the crunching on gravel as he disappeared, leaving her alone and tied up with gunmen.

He pointed to the other man. "Kill the ad. We got what we wanted."

The man did as he was told and sat at the laptop, clacking away, then nodded.

"Now, how about you tell me where the flash drives with the pieces of code are and I'll think about letting you live. We both know you have them and at a secure location."

Anderson would never have bargained with her life. She should be a dead woman either way. Why play games now? He was off and her suspicions on that mountain and in conversation with Bridge back at her safe house were quickly being confirmed.

"I don't have them on me."

"I didn't figure you would. No mind. I'll have them of my own accord in only moments, and with you out of the way, I won't have any trouble retrieving them from your safe house. Yeah, I know about that." His phone rang and he answered, then grinned at Wendy. "I told you I'd have them in no time. Doesn't matter if they're not on you now. They're all in one place and that's all I needed." He spoke into the phone. "You have all of them, I assume… What do you mean? Are you sure?" He growled and ended the call.

"What have you done with Molly?"

He knew. He knew Molly was the missing piece of code. He'd asked about the flash drive pieces, thinking they were all here in Tennessee. He wasn't sure what she'd done with them, but he absolutely knew she'd have Molly. Because of the locket. Wendy had suspected a tracker inside. Too many hits were coming too fast in their exact location. He'd been tracking and updating their whereabouts on the dark web.

Once they arrived at the safe house and Molly went into the bathroom, Wendy had checked the inside of the locket, behind the photo of her father. It hadn't been much bigger than the eye of a needle, but she'd discovered it. And put a plan in place.

He'd tracked the locket to the safe house, as they wanted. By then Amber would have taken Molly to the doctor and then to a hotel. Leaving behind the locket.

He now knew she was missing.

"What have you done with the child?" he asked, venom in his voice.

"Nothing."

"Lies!" He smacked her across the face, then looked at her other captor. "Find her. Now." The figure vanished like smoke, leaving her alone with him. "I know she's the most important piece of the code—embedded in her human flash drive. I also know that putting the code together will create the system to prove you didn't kill Charlie and you hadn't intended to sell the Mask program to the highest bidder."

"No, that's what you're doing. You framed me. And you will never put your hands on Molly." She'd made sure of that. She nor Bridge had any idea what doctor or what hotel Amber Rathbone would use to keep Molly safe. It was best in case torture came into play. And in the spy world, torture always came into play. It wouldn't take a professional long to realize Wendy had no clue of Molly's whereabouts. Didn't mean it would relieve the pain. It could mean a quicker death.

"You sure about that?" he asked.

"I am."

"We'll see." He pivoted and stalked out of the room, leaving her hands bound behind her back and feet shackled. She slipped from the chair to the floor and onto her back. She was raising her legs to bring her arms underneath and back in front of her when a scream shattered the silence and set her teeth on edge.

She knew that voice.

Her heart lurched in her chest and her breath wouldn't come. Another bloodcurdling cry came from the other room and the man returned with a hostage. A bruised and bloody hostage.

Talia.

THIRTEEN

"Who's screaming?" Bridge asked, antsy and ready to storm the castle to rescue Wendy but he had no choice but to be patient and let Wendy do her job, hopefully extracting the confession that would help free her.

Libby removed the earpiece. "I don't know. It wasn't Wendy. He has someone and my guess is he's going to bargain, which means it's someone Wendy knows and cares about."

Talia. He had to have taken her, knowing Wendy would never give up the flash drives without a good reason and Wendy had a soft spot for Bridge, his family, Molly and Talia who had always believed in her innocence.

"I don't think she'll give it up for her," he said. "But I can't say for sure. She knows the job and Talia does too. But it's going to kill Wendy to see him hurt her. Put it on speaker so I can hear."

"Axel doesn't want me to do that, Bridge. You're emotionally invested and, believe me, when you're emotionally invested, you lose sight of the job and bad things can happen." Libby held his gaze, then he glanced at her throat and the long slender scar running across it. She'd never offered up what happened but he was guessing her advice was based on her weakness to someone and it had almost cost her life.

"I'll be okay. I promise. I trust her, and if I go running in, it'll show that I don't. And we might… we might be mending some broken fences between us. I don't want to set us back." He loved Wendy. He'd told himself he'd gotten over her, but his hurt and bitterness had become a mask, deceiving him. Wendy had shown up and the moment he'd laid eyes on her, the truth worked its way up from underneath all the layers of pain.

He hadn't wanted to press on those sore spots but he hadn't needed to. Being in her presence pushed past the trauma to open up his feelings, no matter how hard he'd tried to deny them or ignore they'd been hovering all along.

He loved Wendy Dawson and he always would.

The big question was did she still love him or was she simply trying to right her wrongs so they could be on good terms when this was over? And when it was over, would she leave again? Would she walk away with or without a letter?

He couldn't stomach it.

And if this did go off the rails, he hadn't even

told her the truth. Told her he still loved her and forgave her. That he understood the need to protect loved ones and the hard choices that had to be made. They weren't always the best choices or the right ones, but in that moment, you had to go with your gut and hope for the best and that's what Wendy had done. Yes, she'd fought trusting and relying on others because she'd always had to rely on herself. Or so she thought. But the past couldn't be changed.

Only hearts could change. The present reactions could determine a new future.

And that's what Bridge wanted. More than anything.

Libby turned on the speaker and they sat inside the van listening to Wendy bargaining for Talia's life.

"If you let her go, this won't have to end badly," Wendy said.

"The only one this will end badly for is you," the man said. "What have you done with Molly?"

"Did you think we wouldn't eventually find the GPS tracker in her locket?"

He laughed. "It's taken you this long. It belonged to Adeline. She was always paranoid. Kept that stupid thing in her locket."

How would Anderson know that?

"And how would you know that, *David*?" Wendy asked.

David? David had been behind this? He'd assumed Anderson and so had Wendy. Shock sent a wave through him and his mouth hung open, but Wendy had connected the dots in lightning speed. She must have suspected as much and not revealed it to Bridge since he'd been hired by the man.

But it made sense. David Wingbender was the only other person who would have known about the locket and shared it with Anderson.

He laughed. "So you do know who I am," he said without the modulator. "Molly's mom and I had an affair many years ago. It was brief. She wanted more than I could give and then she had an accident."

An accident or a staged one? He'd make sure it was looked into by local law officials when this was over.

"You trusted the wrong man, Nanny Wendy."

Bridge knew that was going to sting since she'd been dealing with all the trust issues with him and his team. But he felt a sting too, knowing he'd been hired by a man who used him to get to Wendy and ultimately the pieces of code.

When had David discovered Molly was the missing piece of code? He must be in this with Anderson and he was trying to keep himself hidden from Wendy.

"You put a hit out on me?" Wendy asked. "Or was it Anderson? Where is that wily monster? Having you do his dirty work so he can keep his hands clean?"

"Of course I did. Botched a fake kidnapping too to set it all in motion. Brought in a team with the man you love. I knew it would draw you out. And I knew that Mr. Spears would pick Bridge due to his horse expertise. Why do you think I chose a horse camp? For being a spy, you're not that smart."

"Smart enough to know about that locket and hide Molly where you'll never find her."

All this time David had acted like he had no tech skills but he could have doctored the footage.He had access.

"We have to storm the castle, Libby. He might kill her,"

"We can't bust in until we know if David is working alone or with Anderson," Libby said. "We need proof and Wendy knows this. Trust her, Bridge. She knows what needs to be done."

That's when a spray of bullets rammed into the side of the van.

David removed the mask and the modulator underneath it. "How long have you known about the locket?"

"I suspected on the mountain. How long have you known she was the last piece of missing code?" She kept him talking and hoped Talia could free herself from the restraints. She was tech support but even they had some training in self-defense and escape tactics. No wonder Talia hadn't answered her last text from Wendy. David had her.

"When I heard you'd returned to the States. You were seen in Tennessee. I've had people chasing and tracking you all the way to North Korea and then I wasn't sure what happened to you. Thought maybe they killed you. Wasn't sure what to do next, so I sat on it. My brother was always known as the brilliant one. But he was weak. And too honest. I tried to explain the fortune we could make selling the Mask to the highest bidder. But he didn't want it in anyone's hands but America's. As if they wouldn't abuse it too. He was an idealist. Me? I'm a capitalist."

"You're a murderer."

"I didn't mean to kill Charlie. We got into an argument as he finished the project. Anderson was coming to take it and I had one last ditch effort but Charlie refused. It got heated and I killed him. It really was an accident. So I had a short window of time to make a deepfake using you. I knew you weren't a real nanny. My brother might have but he was so oblivious to anything going on except his work. You talked Russian to the gardener and then Spanish to the house-keeper. Could you be multilingual? Sure. I suspected you were here to steal the Mask program. Either way, framing you made it easy on me. Anderson never believed any different. I don't always let people in on my own little secret."

"And what secret is that?"

"I'm as smart as my brother. I created the deepfake, ran to Anderson when I saw his chopper land and told him the nanny had killed Charlie and took the laptop with his work on it. Anderson saw the video and he believed it. He saw you with literal blood on your hands."

"I tried to resuscitate him!" David's sick game had ended with Anderson burning her. All this time she thought he was the bad guy. Thought he was sending operatives after her, but it was David and all his money—and Charlie's money. Billions of dollars he had access to in order to hunt her down. Find the flash drives to sell them. Except he hadn't realized Molly was the last piece. "How did you know it was Molly?"

"You took her on the run with you instead of leaving her. The only reason you'd do that was because she was a piece of code. The last and most important piece. My brother was smart but stupid. Not that I ever cared about the kid." He looked over at Talia, his eyes dark. "Now, I can hurt this woman or kill her or you can tell me where Molly is. I don't want to hurt the child. This isn't her fault. I just want her to give me the code and then I'll send her back to boarding school. She'll grow up and have everything she wants. She'll be safe."

Molly might be safe. Wendy didn't believe David would hurt his niece, and Molly would give him the code. She trusted him. But she wouldn't be loved. And that was no way to grow up. Besides, Molly needed someone who not only loved but understood her. Could help her grow into the adult she was meant to be. The person God created her to be.

"I can't give her to you, David."

"Then I can't promise Miss Dean will be alive for much longer." He wrenched Talia's hair back and put a blade to her neck, nicking it. A fat drop of blood bubbled to the surface. She couldn't help Talia.

"Don't listen to him, Wendy. Keep Molly safe." He pressed the blade harder into her tender flesh and she cried out again. "Don't tell!"

David smacked her across the face and Wendy winced. How was she going to get her and Talia out of here alive?

She couldn't. But she wasn't in this alone. A whole team was on her side. God was in this. She had to trust all of them for help.

But they needed to hurry. Time was running out.

"Ambush!" Bridge yelled and he and Libby ducked. They wore Kevlar vests but that wasn't going to protect their heads or extremities. They were in a tin can being shot at. Bullets slammed into the van and shattered windows up front, the sound deafening. Outside the van they had no clue how many shooters were out there or where, but they could not stay here. "I'm going out and toward the cabin. Cover me."

"On your six. Go!" Libby called and Bridge slid open the side van door, revealing woods all around. The bullets had come from the opposite direction, and he hoped no one was lying in wait in this direction too, or he and Libby would never make it to the cabin.

He jumped out, his heart beating wildly in his chest as he raced into the woods, Libby was right behind him like she promised and returning fire. A buzzing came from above. He knew that sound.

"Drone. Military grade," he hollered as they took cover among the trees and bramble. Snow stuck to their shoes and pant legs, wet from the earlier rain.

Libby ran from the bush and aimed her rifle as more bullets rained down from behind them and above. She fired and the drone broke into pieces and fell from the sky. "Keep going. Move!"

Bridge bolted into action and they raced through the woods, the gunfire falling back but not ceasing. His lungs burned and his calves were on fire as he kept up with Libby's super-sonic pace. Did the woman have bionic legs?

She was faster than lightning but he ran with her, staying right on her tail as they raced toward the cabin. They'd outrun the gunmen, but they also knew where they were headed. Knew this cabin. It was only a matter of time before they descended and the whole place was surrounded. They couldn't wait for more confessions or hostage negotiations. They had to go in now. Fast.

"I have eyes on David Wingbender," Libby said. "He's got Talia in his grasp and a knife to her throat. I'm taking the shot."

"Take it."

She put the scope to her eye. Aimed. Fired.

The bullet slammed through the window, shattering it. Talia shrieked and David Wingbender went down dead. Bridge and Libby flew inside the cabin. Wendy spotted him coming from the back door and sighed.

"I guess you know it wasn't Anderson, but David. He made it look like I'd killed Charlie. Anderson burned me and it was legit in his eyes. He did see me with blood on my hands."

"I know," Bridge said, slipping the key from her pants button and unlocking her feet, then cutting away her zip ties while Libby helped Talia to her feet and freed her as well.

"You know David's an idiot. You never secure hands in front," Libby remarked and held up Talia's zip ties. "You okay?"

Talia nodded. "My neck."

"I know," Libby said softly. "You're alive though, and it could have been much worse. We have to go. Whoever he's got working for him—mercenaries if my guess is right—they're going to be here any second and it's going to end in a blood bath."

"I need to call Anderson. Turn myself in and we have the audio."

"You got audio?" Talia asked and threw herself on Wendy, hugging her. "How on earth?"

Wendy pointed to her collarbone. "Spy gadgets. Your favorite."

Talia laughed. "I can't believe I can even laugh but I do love a good spy gadget. David left keys to the SUV outside. Y'all can use it to drive us out of this place and somewhere safe."

"Perfect."

Bridge grabbed the keys and they raced outside toward the black SUV sitting in the drive.

Talia stopped abruptly. "Wait! The laptop. He has your videos and the deepfake on Charlie's laptop he stole when he said you took it. We need it. I'll be right there. Go!" She darted inside before Bridge could protest. They might not have minutes. They might not have seconds.

"Start the engine," Libby said. "Turn this around so we can speed out of here if we need to."

"Right. Yeah."

"Wait," Wendy said. Bridge looked at her in the rearview mirror.

"What is it?"

"I never saw Charlie's laptop so when or where did Talia see it if she's a prisoner? And her zip ties were in front, not behind. Libby's right. That's an idiot move...unless she did it herself."

A click sounded.

Bridge hollered, "Bomb!" Libby hollering the same thing.

They opened the doors.

And then a sonic boom hit and a heat wave rolled over them. Bridge felt the impact of the pressure sending him through the air and flying. Debris rained down.

His ears rang and everything sounded as if they were underwater.

Had Wendy escaped? Had she jumped?
Had Libby?

His body landed on the ground with so much force his teeth rattled and then he descended into darkness.

FOURTEEN

Wendy paced the hospital room. Bridge had taken a major hit and fallen on a branch, which had impaled him. He'd needed surgery on his spleen. Thankfully it had gone well and now he was sleeping and medicated.

Libby and Axel entered the room. "He awake yet?"

"Not yet." Wendy had been spared the worst of the explosion. She'd been launched into a snowdrift on one side and Libby on the other. She'd been jarred and rattled and would be stiff for days but she was in one piece.

Talia had run from the cabin right before it exploded. She and Libby had given chase and caught Talia with the laptops. Charlie's and David's. Talia had begged her forgiveness and told her that David had approached her two years ago. He'd offered her a lot of money to reveal any information on you and had sweet-talked her, then began a romantic affair. She thought he loved her and things spiraled out of control, but Wendy didn't buy it for a second. She had been wrong. Her judgments had been wrong. All skewed due to her lack of trust and the overwhelming feeling she had to bear her burdens alone. She supposed Talia being a woman had softened her but women could be as cruel and monstrous as men, and sometimes more so.

Either way, looking back, she should have told Bridge what had happened and allowed him and people he knew and trusted to help. He was the one person she actually could trust. She might not have done six months in a torture chamber in North Korea. But she had drawn close to God in those moments, felt his presence in her life. And yet the moment she gained her freedom, she went right back to her old ways, relying on herself. Why had she done that? Why did anyone do that?

Forgetfulness maybe. Sometimes after bad situations people forgot God had been their comfort and provider and as those memories dimmed so did their faith. That's what happened to Wendy. But she was done forgetting. Done believing she was the only person who could take care of herself and others. She needed help and wasn't going to live in fear of asking for it ever again.

She looked from Bridge to Libby. "Are Molly and Amber safe?"

"Yes, they're safe. Amber drove Molly straight to an urgent care in the next town. She has the flu and strep but she's been given medicine and they're at a resort in Splendor Pines, which is only about thirty minutes from here. She's good friends with their sheriff, Rush Buchanan and his wife, Norah. He put deputies on the resort to provide extra protection. Safe house has been compromised and she didn't feel it was safe to return."

"I agree. I'm glad she had some friends nearby. I've actually been to Splendor Pines and stayed at the big resort there. Skied and hung by the fire." Back when she and Bridge were together and a couple. They'd found a sliver of time one winter to escape the daily grind and be together just the two of them. She had savored every single minute of that weekend.

"Amber said Molly's been asking about you and Bridge though. She promised her y'all were safe and was honest with her about Bridge. That he had been injured but the doctors had taken care of him."

Bridge moaned and Wendy hurried to his side. "Hey. Welcome back to the land of the living," Wendy said.

"What happened?"

"You decided to play Superman and fly through the air. Didn't play out so well." She told him about the surgery and that he'd be in the hospital a few days.

"Was it Talia?"

"Yes," Wendy said. "She'd been in on it all along. David had offered her a lot of money and she had a mountain of debt, then to keep her doing his bidding I suspect he played on her singleness and entered a romantic relationship with her. He's a conniving, manipulative man. She was indeed playing double agent, even if she was an analyst. She fed Anderson false information and they used the original Mask program to convince Anderson I was rogue and had been for a while with doctored photos and videos. Anderson believed David because why not? And Talia was my closest ally and Anderson knew it. Talia had even given David one of my messages on her voicemail. He used my voice to craft a message through an AI program that told Talia I'd killed Charlie and was going to sell Mask to the highest bidder. The technology is so advanced, Anderson wouldn't have had anything to prove it wasn't me on that voicemail."

"I want to be surprised but technology is so advanced that I'm not," Bridge said. "And Anderson would have trusted Talia enough he might not have tried to test it for authenticity."

Wendy nodded. "She used a spy gadget to block my calls to Anderson. In those first few months, I'd tried to call him to change his ways, but he never received them and I thought he was ignoring me because he didn't want to hear it. Sometimes technology doesn't work in our favor. Not when vindictive, wicked people have their hands on it too."

"Does Anderson know now? Are you still a fugitive?"

"No. Archer called Anderson and his superior, filled them in on everything that transpired. Axel said to be appreciative of that since Archer hasn't had contact with the agency in over eighteen months. I talked to Anderson this morning."

Axel approached the bed. "She's right. It was a big deal on Archer's part. We gave Anderson all the proof and Talia is recorded admitting the truth."

Wendy's cheeks heated as she prepared to share why Anderson would believe the photos and videos. "Anderson hated to admit he believed it was me but that was my MO—lone wolf—and the proof was there." She brightened a bit to say, "Feels good that I'm no longer a fugitive." And she'd been offered her position back at the Bureau if she wanted it. She didn't.

Right now things were all up in the air concerning her future. Everything hinged on Bridge and his thoughts about Wendy and their future together.

"All those tough guys on the mountain," Axel said, "Talia helped David find mercenaries and she set up the dark web ad with all her tech skills."

"I can't believe I never saw it coming," Wendy said. "You were right, Bridge, and I was wrong. I'm so sorry. I almost got you killed."

Bridge took her hand and tossed her a weak smile. "Please tell me you both heard and will witness that Wendy Dawson admitted to not only her being wrong but me being right."

Axel and Libby laughed. "We heard," Axel said. "We're going to grab a coffee. Give y'all some time alone."

As they left the room, Wendy caught their murmured conversation.

"When are you going to admit I'm always right?" Libby asked.

"Ah, Libbs, you know I'm not a liar. Can't admit to something that's not true."

"One of these days, Axel Harvey Spears, you're going to look me dead in the eye and tell me I was right. And mean it."

"You think?" he asked, amused.

"I know."

They chuckled and then Wendy couldn't hear their words anymore.

Wendy perched next to Bridge. "The money David transferred into Axel's account is going to Molly. Everything that was Charlie's is hers alone. She's a super rich little kid."

"Must be nice." He winked. "I wish she was here to recite facts I don't care about. I miss her."

"She grows on you for sure, doesn't she?"

"She's not the only female that's grown on me."

"You like Libby then?" she teased.

Bridge laughed, then winced at the pain. "No laughs. It hurts. And no, I'm not talking about Libby." His amber eyes met hers, and her belly fluttered and her chest tightened.

"No?"

"No." He tucked a strand of hair behind her ear. "I wasn't sure if you were alive or dead when that bomb went off. All I could think about was that I should have told you I love you. That I never stopped loving you even if I'd convinced myself otherwise."

Wendy's heart soared. He loved her. Yes! "Well, that's good to know because I was thinking I should have told you the same thing. I wanted to prove I trusted you and that I'm done going rogue. That's why I agreed to call your team. I wanted you to know that I not only trust you but don't want to go it alone. Not everything is my problem to carry or fix alone. I can't. It's too much to bear. Would you give me a second chance, Bridge? I've done you wrong, even if

I thought what I was doing was right and convinced myself that it was in your best interest and in your family's best interest. But I miscalculated. Way off. I should have come to you with what happened and allowed you to help. Things might have turned out differently. I know they would have."

"I agree but we can't change the past, Wendy. And God has worked it out for good because He brought you back into my life, and I'm working with a team I love in a job I love. In all the pain, He has been faithful to me. And to you."

"He has." Tears burned the backs of her eyes. Bridge was, per usual, on point. Even in the aftermath of her wrong choices, God had been gracious and merciful. Even in that North Korean prison, God had been with her. Comforted her in ways she had never experienced before and might not again. He was trustworthy. "You have no idea much I love you and thought of you every single day, terrified that you'd moved on and someone else would be kissing you, loving you, having children with you. Hearing you say how much you loved them. It might have been worse than torture. Honest."

Bridge's eyes filled with moisture. "Thing is, Wendy, after loving you, I couldn't imagine loving anyone else. No one could hold a candle to you." He pulled her down close to him. "Wendy, can I kiss you? Properly. Not to be first to walk away but as a way to say I want you to be with me. For as long as God gives us."

Wendy remembered that kiss while he was attempting to break free and away from her. Now he was saying he wanted to be with her and her insides jittered and adrenaline raced. She was actually nervous. She'd kissed Bridge many times but this felt like their very first kiss. And in some ways, it was. "I hope you never stop kissing me, Bridge. And for the record, you don't need permission. Just promise to make it a life-long habit."

"Oh, I can promise you that." He kissed her, with a tenderness that expressed his promise for a lifetime of partnership and faithfulness. She sank into it and savored it, wishing they didn't have to breathe or break away. When she finally needed air, he smiled. "What are you going to do about the spy game now that your name is cleared? You never mentioned the future."

"That's because I needed to hear from you first. You are my future, Bridge. You're all I've ever wanted. Axel has offered me a job. He likes that I'm down to be kicked in the kidneys."

Bridge howled until he hurt again. "He's a sadist."

"I sense that. And I was wrong about Archer. You know he was the old man in the truck."

"Shut your mouth."

She chuckled. "You know I can never do that."

"Don't I though," he teased. "I wonder how many other times he's been around and I never knew it."

"I don't know. I have a feeling he's going to be doing that a lot. Just because he can." She smiled. "So…how do you feel about working together?"

"I couldn't think of a better partner or a woman I trust more."

Wendy kissed him again, loving his lips on hers and the way his scruff scratched at her skin. "Good," she murmured against his lips, "because I said yes."

"I'm going to offer you something else that will require a yes." Behind his eyes the question rang loud and clear.

"Well, don't wait too long." Time had already stolen too much from them. But time had also brought them back together.

"No time like the present then."

EPILOGUE

Three months later

Bridge stood at the horse arena on the Spencer ranch, watching Wendy and Molly race through the barrels. For the past two weeks that's all they'd worked on, gearing up for Molly's first spring race in Austin. She was a natural and Bridge loved teaching her how to ride as much as he loved their walks to the pond in the evenings to fish. She was good at that too and never forgot her mistakes, which meant she never made them twice.

As soon as Bridge had been released from the hospital, they'd raced to Molly and brought her back to the ranch here in Texas and began making wedding plans. Nothing long and drawn out, and he hadn't needed to buy a new ring, because she'd kept it locked up at her Bear Valley safe house all these years, unable to let it go.

A week later they were married right here on

the ranch and now she wore a sparkling wedding band along with her engagement ring. She was now Wendy Spencer, his wife and partner in all things.

Now, as Bridge watched the two riders he loved, his two brothers stood beside him. Stone, his elder brother, sipped a cup of coffee. "Molly's a natural. She's good with Nathan too." He and Emily had a one-year-old baby boy with red hair like their mama and her feisty attitude too. When asked when they planned on a second baby, they gave exasperated expressions and said Nathan required four hands and then some so they weren't sure about baby #2, but Bridge caught the teasing in their voices and suspected sooner before later.

Rhode, his younger brother, leaned on the fence on his other side with his two old Labs sitting beside him, tongues out, watching Molly and Wendy race. His twins were climbing the fence, hoping to make it over and into the arena before their dear old dad could stop them. They were three and a half now and as buck wild as ever. Molly wasn't as fond of River as she was Brook, because River was pretty rowdy and in Molly's personal space more than she liked. His wife, Teegan, was pregnant again with another set of twins. They were in panic mode pretty much 24/7 and he looked at Rhode and chuckled. "I see some gray coming in there, Cowboy."

"Yeah well, raise a set of twins who only know Mach speed and have sticky fingers, then talk to me. Oh and another set on the way. Molly is the most well-behaved child I've ever met. I wish you complete and total mischief-makers when y'all decide to have kids. It'll be my gift to you."

Bridge was ready for a baby, and he and Wendy had discussed it.

Since Molly had lost her guardian, Bridge and Wendy were fostering her and the adoption process was in progress. They'd set up a trust for her and used some of it to buy her a horse and a Shetland sheepdog. She'd named him Oxford and he and Wendy thought it was pretty fitting considering the kid had the entire Oxford Languages dictionary memorized. Bridge often asked her to recite it to Rhode, teasing his brother with the hope he might gain a vocabulary above a sixth grader one day.

Wendy hadn't gone to work for Spears & Bow after all. Molly had been traumatized and Bridge's sister, Sissy, had been working with her, counseling her, using her Cavalier spaniels, Lady and Louie, to assist. Wendy wanted to stay home and take care of her for a while and then maybe ease back into work part-time or be a mom herself. Bridge was on board with both ideas. Whatever she wanted. As long as they were together. And Axel said the door was always open, and Wendy had offered behind-the-scenes work on a new case that had developed. Right now, Axel wasn't sure they'd accept or not until they'd vetted the man who had requested their protection services.

The case was local and hit close to home for Axel. In his FBI days, a vicious serial killer had murdered Axel's wife while Axel had been working the case, closing in on him.

The FBI had questioned a local Texan and declared him a person of interest which had caused a lot of threats and he wanted a man on the case who knew the case. Who knew this killer better than Axel?

But Axel was unsure due to the emotions it brought up. Bridge had no idea what he'd do either if he was in Axel's shoes. He was glad his wife was alive.

"Dinner is ready," Mama called as she propped Sissy's and Beau's little girl, Sabrina, on her hip. She was only a little over a year and the spitting image of Sissy, therefore Rhode too since they were twins. "Y'all come eat these tamales while they're hot!"

Wendy and Molly dismounted and jogged toward them. Stone and Rhode and the dogs were already at the kitchen door.

"Molly, wash your hands and then you can eat, okay? You did a great job today." Wendy smiled and wrapped her arm around Bridge's waist.

"Okay. And I know. I'm a very good horse rider."

She hurried on ahead. When they'd asked her if she wanted to be adopted by them and become their daughter, she simply said yes. But the excitement was in her eyes and her stimmed hands.

Bridge looked down at Wendy. "This is all I ever wanted, Wendy. To be married to you. Live near this ranch. Having Molly is amazing. I've never been happier." He kissed his wife and drew her close.

"Never?"

"Never."

A sly grin slid across her face. "I think I can make you happier." She patted her belly.

He paused and looked at her belly, then held her gaze. "Are you serious?"

"Yep. I found out this morning. I was waiting for the right time and here and now when I prove you wrong—that you've never been happier—seemed like the perfect moment." She laughed as he picked her up and twirled her in the air, planting a kiss on her lips.

"I don't even care that you're devious about timing. I love you."

"I love you too. And you know twins run in your family so…" She grinned and shrugged.

Twins. "As long as you're my partner, bring it on."

* * * * *

Don't miss Jessica R. Patch's next book,
Threat of Revenge,
*part of the Dakota K-9 Unit
continuity series,
available in August 2025, wherever
Love Inspired Suspense books are sold!*

*And look for more books in
Jessica's Elite Protectors series,
coming next year!*

Dear Reader,

Sometimes, we don't realize we're trying to do everything alone. But our actions certainly reveal it. Wendy had been so used to trusting in only herself she didn't recognize she wasn't allowing anyone else to help her or share in her burdens, not even God. I hope you'll reflect on your own lives and ask God to help you recognize any areas where you feel you're in it alone, and let Him comfort you and bring aid only He can. I would love for you to join my monthly newsletter, Patched In, and receive my exclusive gift to you: a free short psychological thriller. You can sign up at: https://jessicarpatch.com/subscribe/

Warmly,
Jessica